Arte Publico Press
Houston, Texas

This volume is made possible by a grant from the National Endowment for the Arts, a federal agency, and the Texas Commission for the Arts.

Arte Público Press
University of Houston
Houston, TX 77204

Rodríguez, Joe, 1943-
Oddsplayer / Joe Rodríguez
p.   cm.
ISBN 0-934770-88-3 : $8.50
1. Vietnamese Conflict, 1961-1975—Fiction.   I. Title.
PS3568.034878034   1988   88-10484
813'.54—dc19   CIP

For Frank Louis Rodríguez
and J.D. Rodríguez, Sr., SKC, USN

1

At the horizon an unseen sun bled into morning. The howitzers were finally silent and shrouded shapes became recognizable—not distinct but isolated against consciousness. The sentries who had crouched through the night searching the dark loosened their grips on their weapons, thumbed the safeties and dared believe that they were survivors. The morning light was a reprieve.

Hendrick leaned against the rear wall of the outpost and tried to stamp the chill and stiffness from his legs. The jarring of his boots against the wood drummed like gunfire far off. He caught himself thinking of home, no longer aware of the barbed wire perimeter. Forcing himself awake, he kept watch through the small opening of the bunker, fighting the exhaustion which rose in his throat like vomit.

Isaacs remained behind the machine gun, his head turning slowly as he searched the arid terrain fronting the outpost. He had taken off his helmet, and his bulky flak-vest dwarfed his head making it a clear target. Hendrick's eyes closed—impacting bullet, rush of blood, the spasms of someone shot through the skull. He jerked awake, looked out and was cold. Violent death was crowding him.

Before Isaacs noticed his own ragged breathing, Hendrick moved to a corner away from the light and lit a cigarette. The smoke flattened out against the low roof of the bunker in vague broken spirals. Hendrick let the match burn its length watching the flicker while someone went up in flames. He blew out the glare and crushed the scrap between his fingertips. Letting himself slide down the burred wooden walls, he sat down and threw the burnt fragment at the dim back-lighted bunker opening. The charred remnant failed to reach outside. He heard it fall back against his flak-vest. Wiping the ash against his musty uniform, he listened detached and indrawn; he smoked cupping the fiery glow and tried not to think.

"It was a bush—only a bush." Isaacs turned to him and then looked back at the barbed wire.

"What time is it?" Hendrick asked quickly, to keep Isaacs calm.

Isaacs twisted his watch down against his wrist. "Near five."

"Christ," Hendrick said wearily and crushed his cigarette against the sole of his boot. "Twelve hours. It's been a long watch."

"Flares were up everywhere. When I heard the rockets and mortars, I thought we were dead."

"Let it rest, for Christ sake," Hendrick said angrily. "It's morning."

"How?" Isaacs asked. "Flares and gunfire. Four months, a year—it makes no difference. Death was outside the barbed wire, nothing else. No God. Not a memory of home."

"Why talk?" Hendrick asked. "Even Talbot fears an attack. All we can do is play our hand."

"In the dark, trying to pray, I felt trapped in a nightmare. I clutched for the other side of sleep. But I could not wake. Morning means nothing except a clear target. I stink of mildew and scared sweat. What remains?"

"You're a friend, Isaacs, and I can't figure you. You never lived where the fighting is up front. Home and the wire are the same. Think with your skin. Don't let your head be a target."

———

The dust from armored vehicles and patrols settled in the night's uneasy stillness and now the air was cool and fresh.

The mountains to the northwest had not yet caught the sun and they were primal shapes. Daybreak—one more test was over and the camp came to. Inside the rows of tin-roofed plywood huts, men fought their way to consciousness and then moved sluggishly to resume the war. They crawled out from their wooden cots, shivered in the cold dampness and waited for discomfort to drive them to decision.

The sentries were ordered finally from the sandbagged wooden outposts that ringed the camp. They assembled near the command bunker. Machine guns were carried back to the armory to be checked in and stored for the next watch. When the gunners returned, every man came forward and put his flares and grenades into separate boxes stacked in the dust. Latched shut, the marked cases were taken to the armory where the contents were counted. Only if the count was right would the men be dismissed.

While they were waiting for word, the men stripped the magazines from their rifles and smoked in the open. No one gave warning that the top sergeant was walking toward them. The men in the front cued the numbers in the rear, threw down their smokes, and began lining up precisely. Talbot ordered the group to attention and opened the formation. At another command, each man brought his rifle up to his chest, and the bolts were thrown open. Forgotten cartridges were ejected and arced to the ground while the guilty tried not to give themselves away.

"Only twenty-three days left, you stupid bastards," someone cursed.

"Clear your weapons on post, meatheads. Shoot yourself," another spat out.

Talbot eyed the wrongdoers in the ranks as he inspected them. The men quieted down but the silence was tense. The first sergeant barked and rifle bolts slammed shut and triggers were pressed. Firing pins snapped into place. As the formation brought their rifles down beside them, the thick canvas slings slapped noisily against the wooden stocks. The sound carried sharp in broken unison and then echoed a cracking dissonance. At last, the previous attack close by was explained to quell rumors. Then the men were dismissed. Drained but alive, they walked back to their hootches. Time or date were meaningless. One more day was beginning, one more night was past.

Hendrick and Isaacs walked to their hut, helmets at their sides. Isaacs kept quiet because he knew that Hendrick would say nothing now that they could be overheard. Hendrick grew up in north Chicago. He did not discuss whether people were good or bad. In a city someone is not right and can hurt you. Think quick and use crowds for cover. No one in the camp could be trusted. The soldiers bettered their chances if someone else lost out. Play odds for survival and everything is for sale. If someone spoke against Talbot, such information could be traded for an easy job or a less dangerous assignment.

Both men were young but their faces were haggard from the lack of sleep. Isaacs stopped at one of the spigots spaced at intervals within the confines of the huts. He turned the faucet handle to see if the water was running. The pipe bucked noisily and rusty liquid spewed onto the bed of rock and gravel that channeled the flow deep into the impermeable earth. Isaacs let the water run, washed the film of dust from his hands and face, and then drank the cloudy fluid from his palms. When he finished, he splashed water on the back of his neck to wash off the chafing dust. The wetness soaked into the sweat. He refilled his canteens and Hendrick took his place.

Hendrick worked at his canteens, hung them back on his utility belt, and then rolled up his sleeves. "Talbot's coming," he said as he leaned down to wash his hands and arms.

"Toward us?" Isaacs asked in a low voice.

"Yes." Hendrick squeezed the water from his arms with his thumbs.

"Bad news," Isaacs said, and kept his eyes down.

"He might have heard us last night," Hendrick answered.

"We would have heard him," Isaacs whispered and his voice shook.

"Talbot turned up behind me once on watch. I never heard him. I don't know how long he was there. I jumped and swung my rifle. He grabbed the barrel and laughed, then left without a word. I had never heard him laugh but that sound . . ." Hendrick cupped his palms and drank.

———————

Sergeant Talbot passed Hendrick and Isaacs, ignoring them. He had other matters on his mind. He cut through the rows of huts, his well-shined boots crashing into the elevated boardwalk that was dry ground when the monsoon came. Stopping at the first hut in the row of quarters closest to the command bunker, he slammed inside. Kirsch, the medic, was sweeping the front room in the dispensary, but Talbot did not wait for him to turn around. "Delta Company was hit last night."

Kirsch turned around, leaned his broom against the plywood partition that divided off the room and held his ground. He was a naval enlisted man, a hospital corpsman assigned to the Marines. "I saw the flares. How many casualties did they take?"

"One KIA; twelve wounded," Talbot announced. "Seven of them had to be medevacked out by chopper. Delta was lucky. Only one of the rockets fell on living quarters. The raid was quick; the rockets first. The gooks didn't try to breach the perimeter in force. That raid makes four attacks on units spread all around us. We'll be next. Then we'll see."

Kirsch seized the broom and turned away from Talbot.

The top sergeant ran the whole camp except for the dispensary. The corpsman was not just another foot soldier, a grunt under Talbot. Kirsch reported directly to the commanding officer of the post.

"We're here to fight," Talbot said to the back of the other man. "Our job is to engage the enemy. That's what we're paid for."

"I'll do my job," Kirsch said as he walked away.

"Your job! Fuck your job. You go out to those scrap heap villages once a week and pass out medicine and supplies that those yellow bastards pass off to the same black-pajamaed slants that hit Delta."

Kirsch whirled around and faced the top sergeant. "Only children, women and a few old men are left in those villages. They need everything I give them for themselves. All they want to do is grow their rice where the earth doesn't stink of napalm and get back their own country before we blow it all to hell."

"The generals should call down artillery on those dung heaps or send down jets and smear those two-faced yellow kikes around the countryside. The village between us and Delta should be ashes right now."

"How do you know the rockets that hit Delta were fired from Four-Miles? If you attack those villagers, every person for twenty miles will turn against us."

"Turn against us?" Talbot snorted. "None of those dinks help us and that means they're already against us. Those slopeheads know when their fathers and brothers are going to stick it to us. When have they ever given us a warning of an attack?"

"If the local people tell us anything about strangers in their village or about troop movements, then their own countrymen waste them. If they refuse to cooperate with us, then we burn them out of their homes. Staff Command tells the people to take their lives in their own hands. But the villagers have no real choices about what to do with their lives. Everything we tell them is a fraud."

Talbot put his hands in his back pockets and threw his shoulders back. Kirsch was no naval officer, just a hospital corpsman attached to the Marines. "Fraud is a two-bit word that a shill uses when he's bet wrong. They have to play odds just like the rest of us. I don't know why the War Department attaches naval personnel to the Marines. All of you are sea-lawyers or bleeding-hearts."

"The Marines get Swabs because you need a few people with average intelligence and not just over-active glands."

Talbot's hands came out of his pockets and he glared at Kirsch, his jaws tightening so that the muscles in his face were knotted. Kirsch did not falter and the air was full of hate.

"You received the medical supplies that you requisitioned?" barked the top sergeant.

"Yesterday. There was less than I ordered, but everything came through. I have enough bandages, splints and intravenous fluids now for heavy casualties. But we need more litters and, more important, we need another corpsman."

"Put in another requisition for the litters, but forget the extra pill-pusher."

"If we take heavy casualties, someone will die before I can reach him," Kirsch said angrily.

"Then you'll have to do your job twice as fast as you think you can. The men are drilled in first aid. You saw to that. Anyone can slap on a bandage." Talbot smiled thinly. "The men can take care of themselves or even another grunt, if they have to."

Kirsch had heard Talbot before. "I can't cover a hundred men spread out over this compound," he hurled back. "If this camp is attacked in force, no one else will have time to take care of the wounded. Every man will fend for himself and someone badly injured will be left on his own."

"Let me worry about the casualties," Talbot answered contemptuously. "Just do your job, Kirsch."

The corpsman's eyes narrowed and his fists clenched at his sides. But he caught himself, saw what Talbot was trying to do to him and hooked his thumbs into his back pockets. "I can still use Hartman," he countered.

"Take him. He's no use to me. Hartman is too occupied with ghosts. I need fighters, not hair-shirts cringing from this war or doubts about themselves." Talbot turned abruptly and walked to the rear of the hut talking as he left. "Just be ready, Kirsch. Our time is close. Be ready or you'll be one of those ghosts that Hartman can't put to rest."

"I'm not Perez or a prisoner that you can lock in a back room," Kirsch hurled at Talbot's back. "I know how to keep my head down."

Talbot stopped as if he had been struck. "Perez was a stupid Spic, but he had balls. The prisoner withheld information. I made her talk."

"Yeah," Kirsch answered. "You persuaded her to cooperate, just like you shipped Perez north."

Talbot went silent for a moment. Kirsch heard a choked, guttural sound.

"I'd send you north into full combat, you traitor's prick, if I could. You're bad for my men. They laugh at me behind my back because I have no authority to transfer you." Talbot slammed his fist into the door knocking it off one set of hinges and smearing blood on the painted wood stripping. Then he walked out, kicking the door ajar behind him.

The helicopter was taking fire; even over the roar of the rotors, bullets cracked and whined. The pilot made the craft skip like a stone while it swerved from side to side. Perez felt his whole body quivering and his insides slammed against his ribs. The craft angled down steeply and he braced himself for the impact. At the last moment, the nose of the chopper snapped up and thick dust billowed as the craft bounced hard and then settled in.

"Go, go," the door gunner shouted and pushed him out. He stumbled and thrust the butt of his rifle against the earth in order to keep his balance. Two stretchers were rushed toward the chopper.

Someone had one arm and was pulling him down and rushing him away from the wash of the rotors. "Let's go," a voice shot back at him and the man raced ahead and dove into a foxhole. Perez tried to shake out of his field pack, but the Marine grabbed him and yanked him into the pit. "Jesus, mother-fucker, you want to die quick. Brace up against the dirt for the incoming."

He heard the motor rev up fiercely and the chopper shot upward. Then there was a sharp explosion and the air hissed over the foxhole. The next blasts seemed right at the lip of the trench. Perez flattened against the earth and smelled the hot, rancid dust.

As Talbot strode to the farthest arc of barbed wire that marked off the perimeter of the camp, he tried to put his rage against Kirsch into words. Too many suspicions about all his underlings crowded his thoughts. I asked for troops, he said to himself, not bleeding hearts that are worthless because of fear and indecision. Talbot wrapped his handkerchief more tightly around his injured hand and clenched his fist to draw the pressure firm. Kirsch was weak and would not bear up under the gun. What did that fool think about? How could he forget that everyone outside the wire wanted to see every roundeye dead? Hartman was another coward and he tried to recall what his face looked like, but he could not piece his impressions together. Hartman was a stripling who was panic-stricken when his outpost was overrun. Overwhelmed by fear, Hartman had been jolted out of character and fought courageously. He had lost his head and killed bravely. Talbot wanted to believe that Hartman's awards for valor under fire were flukes. But such an explanation did not ring true. Talbot would have to make sense of a man he had no means to explain.

"Corporal Hartman reporting for duty, Sergeant Talbot." Talbot had pointed the new man to a seat and leafed through his record. A good record, he had thought, and looked at Hartman closely. "You've had your share of front-line action, Marine. No one can grudge your transfer."

Hartman was young, but his face was gray from exhaustion and he moved with the deliberateness of someone who was very old.

"It's war." Talbot paused to measure what effect he was having on the younger man. "You've done your part."

"My part . . ." Hartman seemed to be looking through Talbot, as if he were not there. "Yes, sir."

After Talbot dismissed the corporal and the new man left the office, the top sergeant was left with nothing concrete to make a judgment about the unknown soldier. Talbot came to the unsettling conclusion that he himself had said what he had intended and that Hartman had said what was required, nothing more. The world was slipping slowly out of reach and there were dark warps and unfamiliar signs.

When Talbot had had to take emergency leave and return to the States for his mother's funeral, he felt uncanny—out of place. In two days, he crossed from one side of the world to the other. Two days took him back eighteen months to when he had last seen his native country. When he landed at dusk, he was struck by the numbers of people with white faces and round eyes out in the open so casually, the countless number of cars, the unending parade of neon lights. It was the colors, Talbot imagined, flashing at him everywhere, that made him feel so odd. He was used to a war all of one hue.

Without warning, months ago Talbot had been called to the Old Man's office while he himself was preoccupied with the disposition of his men and the firepower they could bring to bear at each sector of the perimeter. Talbot was prepared to talk numbers and casualties, but not that manner of death. The Old Man was blunt and matter of fact. The colonel brought up how many days leave Talbot had accrued. There was no opportunity for Talbot to tell his superior that going to his mother's funeral meant nothing to him. The Old Man expected his first sergeant to take leave and return to the States, and Talbot could not refuse. He hated being compelled to do something that was a waste of his time. But he was military and he played by rules and rank. He was caught up in a series of events over which he had no control. Many years had gone under the bridge since he had seen her last. He sent her a small allotment each month. Her being on relief would make him look bad.

Talbot could not accept that she had conceived, much less bore him. The thought of such a connection between them was unaccountable. It amused him somehow to imagine her sweating him into life. She had made herself as vague as shadows to him, saying nothing to him of herself, leaving him always in the dark.

How easily Hartman blended with shadows. Talbot never saw him unless he searched. Hartman was always moving in the background out of scrutiny. Did he intend to be so evasive? Talbot had decided that the new man had something to hide. Hartman obscured himself too well. The few times that Talbot accosted him, he was military and correct. But it seemed to Talbot that the younger man looked at him strangely as if he were confusing Talbot with someone else.

"You know this man?" Talbot had asked a sergeant in Hartman's section.

"No," answered the staff sergeant. "He does his job; I've never had any trouble with him."

That's not what I mean, Talbot thought. "I mean what kind of man is he?"

"He does his job, top. Do I need to know anything else?"

How do you place a man who uses silence like a mask? There were men he could not figure out, like Perez or Hendrick. But with those grunts, he could sense the hostility and resentment they barely kept under control. He had no feel for them as people. But their antagonism told him where they stood. Make subordinates hate you and you had them under your control. You had their constant attention. They would pay attention to every move you made and take everything you said seriously. A man in authority must necessarily stand alone.

"My part." Talbot turned his attention to the inflection of Hartman's first few words. Why was that pretty-boy with the blank eyes such a bogey man to him? Talbot let his worst suspicions take hold of him. Was Hartman another candy ass that brought his conscience to combat? Or was Hartman measuring his superior against suspicions of his own? It's hard for a veteran to talk to spit-and-polish behind a desk. All manner of implications whirled into mind. Talbot could not sustain his questioning. "I am in charge of the camp," he murmured. There was nothing else to say.

Talbot turned his thoughts aside. He searched the rows of barbed wire piled in looped coils along the ground. The wire looked impassable but he knew there was some way through the barbed strands that he could not see. He rechecked the overlapping lanes of machine gun fire from the nearby outposts. On this arc of the perimeter, the ground was level and the towers had been built every hundred yards and placed so that most of the area outside the wire could be covered in tandem. The interlocking crossfire from the machine guns was the only real protection for the towers. Each outpost was anchored on thick legs of timber and raised six feet or more above the ground. A sentry-station was like a box on four stilts, the floor extending outward like a parapet. Sandbags were stacked tightly on the parapet two rows thick on three sides and also on the roof of the bunker.

"You buy time, buy time," Talbot said to himself. The sandbags would stop rifle fire and the fragments from grenades—nothing else. There would be enough warning to alert the camp and throw men into the breach. But if the enemy cut a path through the wire, the towers were a wasted gamble. Forty yards beyond the wire, the ground sloped down into a shallow ravine parallel to the towers. The clumps of dry bushes and the stands of brittle grass that grew beyond the cleared areas hid the gully from sight. From the raised towers, the ravine was where the brush grew more thickly and thinned out into a broken cover of dusty undergrowth that grew back despite the chemicals. Fifty feet out from the wire was the kill-zone. Here, the kerosene and oil-soaked earth choked anything that remained alive.

That ravine. Staff Command should fire the brush or saturate the area with defoliants—agent orange could be sprayed by air. "The enemy could hide an army in there," Talbot muttered to himself and cursed the armchair generals who had built the camp where it stood.

Hartman enlisted in the Marines because he liked their movies and wanted action. He was shipped to war through the airfield at Danang. He and the other grunts were herded from the jet in full battle gear, taken to a bleak terminal and told to wait for assignment to a unit. During basic training and in-transit, he was a number. At the airfield he knew he was a battlefield statistic.

A goat was allowed to roam through the crowded terminal. Certain motions made it rear back and butt whatever stood in its way. Some soldiers teased the animal and, as it lunged, they caught it by the horns. Hartman wondered if they were old timers who had come through.

Hartman's first patrol went out the same day: he was flown north with replacements for a combat unit. The previous company which came from Okinawa, green and untested, was massacred. The unit assaulted their objective according to the book. Everything they did was right. They just didn't know enough and took heavy casualties. No one told them about snipers who carved hiding places into the trunks of trees, about pop-up emplacements where assault rifles waited underground or about booby traps not covered in training.

Before his first patrol, Hartman felt as if something had grabbed him by the head and squeezed so hard he could not remember what he had been taught. He went from spit and polish to combat in one day. Marines in the same flight to Danang were posted to units in the rear. Bodies were loaded aboard the return flight that had brought him north. Who was figuring the odds that he would make his 13-month tour of duty?

The sergeant named Dibbs, who had sent out the patrol, had said daytime belonged to the Marines. The light was full, so the gooks were probably in hiding. The PFC on the point in front of the patrol came to Hartman and held out a cartridge. The way he fixed his eyes on you made you think he knew something you didn't.

"This shell is yours. If we get into trouble and there's no way out, make this last round your best shot. The enemy knows what Sergeant Dibbs does to prisoners."

Hartman could not forget being pinned down by automatic fire on his first mission—face pressed to the dirt, as if it were salvation. The grunt in back was calling for a medic. His heart pounded in his chest and he could not breathe. Incoming rounds slammed into the ground in bursts and the drumming concussion shook his whole body. A pulse beat in the earth. In a frenzy that was somehow clear, Hartman figured, "if my blood beats in time with the incoming, I will be dead."

And he was saying, "you mother-fuckers, not one day," and he started firing magazine after magazine. He helped bring back the KIA who bled to death because the medic could not move in the crossfire. The PFC on the point told him, "you'll do."

Afterwards he wanted to write to his younger brother, but could not find the key. Someone offered a tape recorder and he tried to describe his feelings. The sounds were tinny and the voice unreal. No matter how he tried to start, he lost his way. To cope with the fighting, Hartman stopped trying to talk. The wild man on the point had seen him trying and said too much thinking uncovers a man's head. A skull makes the best target.

"The watch is back," Priest said to Hendrick and Isaacs as they were entering the hut. "How goes the war?"

"Don't say anything," Lieck said to Isaacs and Hendrick with a wave of his arm. "Priest is on another one of his rampages. If you encourage him, he'll just do more tedious moralizing."

Priest shot a finger in Lieck's direction. "Better to moralize than bow down to a rat."

"What happened last night?" Lieck asked the two men,

ignoring Priest. "The camp was on alert half the night. No one slept more than a few hours."

"Delta was hit," Hendrick answered.

"KIAs?" Lieck asked.

"One," Hendrick replied. "Talbot said moderate casualties."

"It won't be long," Lieck volunteered, as he laced his boots. "But I'm not worried."

Priest snorted. "What's that you say, Lieck? When your number is up, then it's up. Good motto for a rat."

"Get off it, Priest. Your father's money and connections didn't keep you out of uniform. Smart people like you confuse themselves with noble talk. What matters is coming off first."

Priest stuck a finger into a clenched fist. "Lieck's Code of Conduct: jam yourself into any hole and make it fit."

"When rockets fall on us," Lieck said to the hut, "Priest will forget right and wrong. You college boys are all alike," Lieck continued. "Full of ideas. But schools don't teach the real world. Say anything you like, Priest, you'll still get sucked along with the grunts."

Priest stuck out his upper teeth at Lieck and scraped his nails against a plywood wall.

"Can it," Hendrick broke in. "We just saw Talbot outside. Do you want to end up like Perez?"

"Perez was a fool," Lieck shot back as he wiped the film of dust from his boots with a blackened strip of cloth. "He couldn't keep quiet. He got what he asked for."

Isaacs raised his head and looked at Lieck. "You testified at the court martial that Perez lost his head and hit Talbot. Perez said that Talbot pulled his dumb Spic routine once too often. You said that you couldn't remember what anyone said."

Lieck turned to Isaacs. "Perez lost his head. There was nothing else I could say."

"How can you hear anything when you're crawling on your belly?" Priest spat out.

Lieck spun around and faced his adversary. "Rumor has it that someone else is being shipped north. Maybe it will be you, Priest."

"I don't want to hear this," Isaacs said and clamped his head in his hands.

"Bootlickers and informers spy on each person in this camp and talk to Talbot. Talbot listens and tells them stories. Rumors spread with the fools who believe they're safe. And the malcontents: we are herded together in one hut so that Talbot can keep a close watch.

Priest went on. "To last a tour, a man keeps quiet and goes along, no matter what. Perez couldn't take Talbot's constant insults about his race. He lost his head and Talbot shipped him to that graveyard in the North."

"Stow it, Priest." Hendrick walked to the rear door of the hut and looked outside. "You and Isaacs don't know when to keep quiet."

Lieck walked slowly toward the door, shaking his head. "You will always be out of it, Priest. The whole world's a prison. Duty, family honor—noble talk is jive. A menial with a conscience won't survive. Survive first, let the rest take care of itself.

As long as Lieck was alive, Priest wanted to kill. Lieck's survive-whatever-the-cost-or-be-eaten was sewer thinking. Rats were everywhere in the camp. Maybe they would inherit the world. There was no place for Priest.

Nothing like Lieck intruded into his family's pictures: the photo albums, the home movies, the framed shots crowding the walls, especially in the trophy den. Pictures of Priest were in the house: fishing trips, Little League—all the times he won awards at school. His parents had stacks of memories. Were those images who he was or a reflection of the family? Did they see him or an extension of themselves? When his parents pored over the old photographs, Priest saw time frozen in black and white. That was then and part of me. And now I'm another person, as well.

Lieck carried on as if he knew something no one else understood. Priest's parents shared a secret and could not let him in on it, although they loved him. The secret had to do with all the snapshots, movies and the expensive frames. When life was good, when the business made Dad money, and Mom developed all the latest film, the family got together in the trophy den. They looked at old times. Dad took a day from work and Mom was radiant.

His parents were happy, Priest merely content with the life they provided for him. Pictures of his achievements in school, in sports and scouts just seemed to fill space with no life of their own. He was congratulated warmly and yet the praise seemed out of touch. Often when the family was together on holidays and the past was brought out, he felt their good feelings were ritual for him.

Soldiers use ritual to cope with death. Isaacs carries photos of his wife and home and looks at them at reveille and at taps, as if he were praying. Hendrick will talk a bit about growing up in north Chicago, the streets drawn-lines with niggers on one side and Poles and Bohunks on the other. Memories of his turf keep Hendrick alert at the wire. Lieck shines shoes, polishes brass and fieldstrips and cleans his M-14 over and over. No one else has time for spit and polish. Gleaming brass draws enemy fire. Lieck stays busy. Cleaning tarnished metal and spit-shining boots is better than the "mind fuck."

Priest rages over some sense of loss that once was home—images from the past are everywhere. In his father's den, pictures of triumph line the walls. Frame after frame in precise rows are set off by the smell of leather easy chairs and a varnished oak floor. When Priest thinks of home, a sort of movie runs through his head and Priest is in it, although the film is out of sync.

Priest and his father kept the studied sort of distance that comes of learning how to be a man. When he was eight and punched a hole in his leg learning to ride a bike, his father patched him up. Priest saw his father's hands shaking. Priest was crying and his pop said, "Now, now, enough of that." When his dad was finished, Priest tried to hug him, and his father tousled his hair instead and told him, "that's a good soldier." He helped him get back on the bike and watched him with a sort of faraway intent look. Then he went away.

Maybe the movie in his head started in jerky frames when he brought tokens into his father's den: report cards, special awards and such. His father was glad and told him, "You'll make the family proud of you." And his words were warm but without touch, so that Priest thought that he had done well but not good enough. Whatever he carried in his hands was double—before he brought it into the room and as he left, like a dead bird in his grasp.

The movie in his head was running full tilt during his last year of high school and his freshman year of college. The war played every night across the TV screen like something far away, and yet the war had come home. The movie played and the familiar pattern of day-to-day life began to unravel.

Protesters appeared outside his father's tool and die business shouting that the company's products made weapons and killed babies. On TV, Priest saw jets dropping napalm; he saw the refugees. Also as he looked at the angry faces of the pickets, he realized how his father felt. People who didn't know him were branding him a war criminal.

Priest's life was mapped out before the war. In the room with his father's past crowding the walls, the two of them plotted his future like points on a grid. They worked out a degree in business for Priest because his father was an engineer. After graduation, the son would join a large firm for the experience, start at the bottom and pay his dues. No riding coattails to success. Then, a partnership in his father's firm. Everyone knew the plan.

The movie was badly scratched and out of focus when he and his father began to argue about the draft and his college deferment. Then the trophy room echoed like an abyss. When Priest looked at the picture albums again, were there cracks underfoot in the shadows?

Priest's father was a self-made man who worked hard for everything he had. Traditional, conservative, moved by his own success, which he believed reflected the greatness of the past; the Old Man talked the same sort of history that Priest learned in high school. Yet the faraway war on TV was real, despite the fact that even soldiers play to a camera.

Tough-minded yet forthright, his father lived by a code of values which made him a success. Priest respected his father's stern talk because he demanded nothing of others that he did not live up to himself. For his father, patriotism fit. Neither one of them could say love. Their connection was as tangible as the trophy den.

Priest's father was a veteran. During the Second World War, he was a non-com with the Army Engineers. Precision tools and pre-fabricated parts raised bridges overnight. Tanks and heavy artillery crossed over the machined metal and traveled to the front where we were on one side and the enemy on the opposite.

After the war was won, Priest's dad came home to the parades, went to college, and started his own tool and die firm. In those days, he reminisced, life in the U.S. seemed open like a frontier. There was a rush of rising expectations, a sort of revolution, and a man willing to work hard and think positive could take hold of the American Dream.

In the well-built, two-story house that his father constructed, with the help of friends who were "comers" just like him, pictures of that era crowded the walls like victory. Especially in the den, with the smells of leather and varnish and the solid feel of accomplishment. His father's high school graduation in cap and gown, diploma held high—the look of a determined youth who knows where he is going. Photos in uniform looking like he had seen ghosts, yet shoulders squared, head up, because he knew his duty. Wedding pictures—the beaming groom too happy for words. A series of photographs at college graduation holding his first-born to the camera, as if a son closed a circle and the future was secure.

In that room crowded with his father's glory, the reel of Priest's movie finally jumped off track. He and his father had talked for months about the war. At first, Priest listened while he looked at the shots in uniform. His father thought the war was right. Priest couldn't follow him and, therefore, let it go at first.

The time came when Priest started saying, "If the war is just, why should I take a college deferment from the draft?"

"You've got a double duty to your country and your family. If you feel you have to serve, take the deferment, finish school first, and then go in as an officer."

And Priest couldn't argue against that position in the beginning. After some thought, he replied that using college to keep out of combat wasn't fair. Using special rules to get your own way wasn't right.

"Using the rules to your advantage is just good business," his father snapped.

"What about those people who can't use the fine print? What about those on the bottom who can't afford tuition to buy their way out," Priest answered heatedly.

"That's the way the game is played. Don't talk like a bleeding heart."

That was the problem. His father's sense of things was disconnected from Priest. There was a chasm between his father's pictures and him. Even Priest's likenesses on the walls were counterfeit—Priest was there, yet the images were not the whole story.

The den echoed strangely. There were moments when they were arguing in a fury and Priest was removed. He was lashing out at his father and yet off to the side feeling dead.

"I can't go to college and take a deferment from the draft. Some poor fool will go in my place."

"Why not?" his father raged in turn. "I didn't work my whole life to risk my family's future in a lottery? What about our plans for the business?"

And Priest screamed, "Your family, your business. What of me? You always talked about right and wrong, said follow your conscience no matter what. I can't decide what's true about the war. So I've got to play fair. If everyone has to put a number in a hat to decide who goes to war, I'll put mine in too."

"Smash the family," his father raged. "Waste a lifetime of work to give you chances I never had." The anger masked the pain of losing a son and finding a world he could not understand.

"I have no choice."

"Then go," his father shouted. "Pack your bags and leave."

The movie broke and the room caved in. Exile was worse than anything Priest had ever imagined. But he would not back down. Never.

As he learned to live without a sense of home, Priest went over his life in freeze frame. Priest's father was like a myth that makes itself come true. Maybe Priest was different from his father. Perhaps the world changed. It could be the myth was never real.

There are voids between what people intend and how

they live, between ideals and action. Priest wondered if he had ever really known his parents or they him.

His mother tried to get Priest and his father to patch things up. Some new feature was running in his thoughts, so when his father and he talked they were calm, but it was like trying to see the old pictures by touch. His father was now a hawk whose fervid support for the war was like going back to the photos he understood. If Priest wanted to, he could join up. And Priest kissed his mother, shook his father's hand, and left for good.

The war was like a baffle cutting off two voices from each other. Dad believed that events sometimes outstrip a person's understanding: yet you do your duty. Priest was caught in a crisis when ideas clash against ideals and patriotism is an escape. Priest was living in a state of seige when the military took him. Caught in a crossfire of generations and values, Priest was wounded before he came to combat. He didn't talk to other soldiers as much as vent his pain. The other troops found their rituals in order to cope with combat. Priest was lost and raging among old pictures that once were home.

Lieck put on his sunglasses outside the hut and wished that Priest would be zapped soon. The fucker was noisy—one quick rocket on his post would be worth a tour. He would volunteer to zip up the loudmouth in a plastic bodybag, even pay for the privilege.

For Lieck the days left in country were like rows of shoes. Forget the smell and the dirty cracks in the leather. You pick them up one by one, and work just fast enough to keep the boss off your back until it's quitting time. You collect your money, try for nookie if you can, but it's back to shoes the next day.

Why was Priest always lipping off about musts or shoulds or oughts? Lieck learned to keep quiet in foster homes and institutions for wards of the court.

Fuck your pity, Priest. I got life straight without the games you well-off jerks learn. You talk out of books and turn shoes into dancing slippers because you want art. People need to pretend that shit ain't shit. Sure it stinks. But I'd rather live up front and get what I can, instead of trying to hide the smell. No matter where you go, there is always some-one standing over you and dead time when nothing's happen-ing. What counts is when your cock is jiving.

Lieck's mother was a seventeen-year-old who opened her legs to be loved. She told her boyfriend she was pregnant, he said by who? and left. Nothing was going to tie him down. Her choices were to have Lieck (his father's name) or an illegal abortion. She read stories in the magazines about women dying from them. Her parents told her to accept her punishment. She dreamed of falling down stairs and having a miscarriage. Afterwards, when she was healthy, she would meet someone who loved her and get married. It was too late to be sorry. Her parents convinced her to place the newborn in a home for the unwanted.

Lieck had shelter, food and clothing but not enough care, not enough touch. The people who staffed the places where he was sent had worked with unwanted kids long enough to forget about making a difference. There were always more kids in the streets. The staff was just doing their jobs.

Sometimes people in the community sponsored parties and, at Christmas, there were gifts. Lieck liked guns and shot monsters from hiding. Sometimes someone took a gun away and asked, "Don't you believe in Baby Jesus, little boy?" And Lieck said nothing, didn't even look up and let his face get him into trouble. He just barely crooked a finger and thought pow. Lieck learned better than to speak his mind. People who carry the keys talk about right and wrong, then go home and fantasize about the babysitter while they hump their wives. But you got to talk their language and keep a straight face or they'll make you an example.

Once he discovered sex, Lieck lived from one fuck to the next. He tried to juggle as many "feel goods" as possible at the same time. Way back when, he was humping four different bitches every day. His balls were dragging, but he was flying high. Even if the ladies were moody or on the rag, and wouldn't give it up, just wanted to talk, zipping around was better than the same four walls and sitting alone.

Without pussy, it's ennui, cuntless anomie. Lieck played crossword puzzles because girls were impressed with big words. He understood all of Priest's fifteen-centers, everything he said. It was just noise. The game played and you were in it, no matter what you thought.

You're so much shit Priest, with all your fucking noise. Everything got handed to him on a silver platter growing up. Lots of people never have a house, so cut the sob-in-the-throat-wringing-hands bullshit. All Lieck believes in is apocalypse.

Come on, mama. I'll tell you anything you want to hear to get into your pants.

The rear door of the dispensary teetered on its remaining hinge and the smear of Talbot's blood was congealing in the heat. As Kirsch looked across the camp, he could see the metal roofing of the huts already beginning to catch the sun. Far off, there was the whine of a jet on some distant mission. Drawn along with the sound, Kirsch tried to lose himself in his work. His hands were shaking. He set the door back in place and went inside the sickbay. Another futile day. He was part of a brutal war. Was that better than being a victim?

Why are you here?

Ordinary life was killing me back home. Day-to-day routine was turning me into a zombie. Death and combat would show what mattered.

In his first days, the war stood out in vivid, disjointed unreality: the encircling barbed wire fences with the high wooden towers placed at intervals in back of them, the stacks of crated supplies, the lots of new trucks parked in tight formations off the pot-holed dirt roads, the piles of spent howitzer casings beside boxes of unfired shells. There were the bleak wooden buildings stretching in formation across the barren earth, tin roofing harshly reflecting light. Everything was dull and colorless, yet radiant. Even the unpainted walls of the huts and the rusting shell casings were luminescent. The whole jumble of objects seared the eyes.

But after a matter of weeks, day-to-day objects became muted and drab; only the tin roofs reflected light with the same intensity. Once shocking, the war became like a painted still life without a sense of perspective. Only the troops remained three-dimensional, loading supplies onto trucks, or unloading newly arrived material with heavy lifts. On the roads, they appeared out of the thick dust, as if stepping out of a frame. As they marched to the perimeter and disappeared into the choking haze, they went from solid to flat in the glare.

I must get this right, Kirsch thought. The camp was a target. Worrying about survival made everyone a casualty. He did not intend to write. Instead, he tried to be so aware of his reactions that he could understand why he had worshipped combat. If he could just understand Talbot, maybe he would understand his welcoming a uniform. Merely calling Talbot's decisions into doubt means treason. Did Talbot once realize that he could die? To cover up his fear, he destroys anyone who blinks under fire. A hint of cowardice deserves death. Is he a desperate man without any belief who lets the military be his purpose for living? Make sense of Talbot and Kirsch could begin to understand why he was at war. We have trapped ourselves here for many reasons and trying to discover why is like volunteering for the point.

What about numbing routine, blurred awareness and tedious fury and alienation? So he wrote, put on paper the stalemate and perverse forgetting. He wanted to address someone, make insights part of himself. A hospital sense of death led to mental ambulance chasing. More was at stake than recrimination. He wanted to resist the urge to make excuses. No clucking noises that were like pats on the head for a bad choice bravely met. Who would listen with the savage equanimity needed to cut through sham.

"Death was not real back home."

"No? Death was pulped animals on freeways. You enlisted to see killing at first hand."

"I wanted to brush my teeth and see the bone under the skin. What happened in combat when violent death was no hospital abstraction? I thought that death made life clear and not just the incomprehension and regret of a terminal patient. War seemed real. Humdrum life did not."

"War was a rite of passage. Once you experienced combat, you would be enlightened. Seeing men die would spur you to make the most of your time."

"My question of death had nothing to do with seeing men kill each other. I was not a non-combatant who patched up the wounded. My hands were dirty. I was part of the disaster because of my thinking before the war. I romanticized death. Fascination with death in the abstract is mental ambulance chasing."

"If my life was empty before the war, combat would not give it meaning. I was confused. I wanted to rise out of ashes but that was myth."

Hendrick turned to his tentmates. "You can't talk when Lieck is in the hut."

Priest got angry. "One by one, Talbot will thin us out."

"We're in his camp, and he's the man. Those are the rules back home. You never had to deal."

"All of us are trapped in this hut like outcasts, but we still can't pull together," Priest said to Hendrick.

Hendrick looked at him. Priest could see what was up and could say so. But he was jumpy and his mouth put him on the point. He wondered why. Both his friend Rebo and Priest had gone to college and both of them were smart. Color and the fact that Rebo was a disabled veteran did not explain why Rebo was quiet and watchful, and Priest exploded. Hendrick figured that Rebo had scars on the outside and they were healed. Priest had a secret wound.

Hendrick sat down on his cot. "What Talbot says is Gospel, like it or not. No matter how many troops want him bagged, no one will do anything."

"And I assumed war meant killing in the open," Priest said. "Portsmouth Military Prison or a billet north never crossed my mind. I knew my number would be called and I was tired."

Hendrick took a key from around his neck and opened his footlocker. He lifted out a bottle, opened it and took a drink. He held the bottle out to Isaacs who made no move. He offered it to Priest.

"No, thanks," Priest told him.

"If I have to listen to your story, you can drink my booze."

Priest took a drink from the bottle. "Damn," he rasped. "That's rotgut." He picked up a canteen and took a quick swallow.

"One hundred and ninety proof medicine courtesy of Kirsch. Good for whatever ails you, even wasted talk."

"Talbot sent you on patrol again. You're going to stand

by, and wait for the next one."

Hendrick took another drink. "I don't trust Lieck but I understand him. You and Isaacs, and Kirsch too, live inside your heads too much. You can't compel behavior by proving bad faith. The men know this war is lost. They want to survive and forget."

"You see war now but were blind before. You'll go back like the rest to playing odds. The ones who scream the loudest go to sleep and dream like everybody else: picket fence, my lovely wife, the kids."

"You always go back to color," Priest replied.

Hendrick screwed down the cap of the bottle. He walked to his footlocker and crouched down.

"Take this," he said to Priest and stood up.

"Where . . .?"

"Take it for Talbot. Frag him. Rig a booby trap—toss it in his cot. Just do it."

"Murder?" Priest took the grenade.

"You've got to do sometimes and only afterwards guess the why."

While other kids were worried about acne, being part of the crowd, and having fun, Isaacs dreamed of being a missionary in Peru. He was going to spread the Gospel and serve. No matter that his looks, clothes and interest in early Christians and their martyrdom set him apart. Sarah's father was a minister and she understood. She and the call to carry the Good News were what mattered to him. Cut off and without friends, he found comfort in the Word: even the Light felt forsaken.

The draft intervened in his mission. Caesar wanted thirteen months and the Lord protects his servants. Being inducted into the service, bootcamp, screaming drill instructors and the constant harassment were emblems for being able to endure trial and deprivation. Sarah and he had planned to marry after his mission to Peru. He proposed once he got his orders for overseas. Registering as a conscientious objector had not crossed his mind when he was drafted. Marrying Sarah was important.

Talbot watched the gawky self-conscious kid who got religion and put him with the other question-marks after three months. Isaacs testified for Perez at his court martial, told the Board that Talbot called him a half-breed Indian and a Spic. Talbot was going to ship Isaacs north, but not so soon as to be obvious.

Isaacs befriended Hendrick when he got moved into the disciplinary hut. Hendrick distrusted people who tried to hide behind a smile. Hendrick and Perez had been tight and Hendrick remembered that Isaacs testified when other men who knew the score said nothing. The kid was too eager to be a saint. But he was good people.

Isaacs could not talk with Priest, who walked away when religion came up. Lieck just rolled his eyes. Hendrick could talk about hymns and Gospel music. The rest he heard as if it were Isaacs' story and he had paid his dues. Isaacs tried not to talk; except that he was a sentry at the front gate when a Buddhist monk in orange and a crowd of villagers came to the wire. The monk sat in the Lotus and prayed for hours. Isaacs called in a report and Talbot said shoot anyone who tries to breach the wire.

The chanting stopped, Isaacs relaxed, and the monk poured gasoline over himself and went up in flames. No one in the crowd put out the fire. Isaacs dared not leave his post. The smell of charred flesh choked him. The monk did not scream: silence was so complete he heard flesh sizzle. Then there was a low sound—a sigh of agony or martyrdom, wondered Isaacs after the shock of the yellow flames leaping from the shriveling skin. He could not call in a report. The smoke brought a response from the camp.

Talbot fired over the crowd's head and yelled, "di di," telling them to clear out in their language. Isaacs saw the hate as they retreated from the shots.

"Maybe we can start a fad," Talbot told him. He left the body for the rats.

The monk's immolation was a sign without a key. Everyone became the enemy: the woman who does the laundry, the kid who sells cokes out of a rusty bucket with cloudy ice. Talking about God seemed sacrilege. Spreading the Word could not balance living under siege.

By the time Isaacs was eligible for R&R, the unreal break between stints of combat when no one talks of dying, he was a casualty.

"Don't worry," his wife whispered in their hotel bed in Hawaii. She stroked his face in the darkness. "I hear the war in your voice. I love you. Just holding you is fine."

Isaacs held her tight and wept. "I feel like something in me died. I don't feel whole. God is in hiding and I don't know who I am."

"Your last stand, halfbreed," Talbot told Perez after he hit him. Talbot took out his black book and wrote Perez up. Talbot's words meant north, full combat and death—again the sharp thump and rolling concussion of the incoming.

Word-player Maria had called him. When he talked his words were like hiding. Dirt scraped under his nails and he splayed his free hand. He thought he heard her mutter at the professor under her breath—again the same expression and he was sure. Four adjacent weeks in history and the two of them had not spoken a word. After the hour, when she reached to get her books, he touched her arm and asked what she had said.

"Cochinada académica," she replied.

"What?"

"Academic bullshit. The instructor has his facts color-coded. The Treaty of Guadalupe Hidalgo was forced on Mexico at gunpoint and Chicanos have been beating time ever since."

They rasped like bare metal.

"Perez, *Pérez*—you don't speak Spanish: aren't you Chicano?"

"I'm Mexican American." Later she would remind him of the name he picked to stay invisible and question his claim: "I'm American." She laughed and held out her arm next to his. "Your skin is bronze like mine. How are you going to talk around that?"

He felt taps on his shoulder.

"The incoming has quit for now. But let's wait a few minutes for mad rounds."

Perez scratched at the soil and watched the loose powder sift down the wall of the foxhole. Sandbags filled with earth circled the rim.

"I'm Cooper," the private said.

"*Pérez*," he responded and kept still, since Cooper made no move.

"Another Spic," Cooper said, smiling. He looked at Perez and stopped. "Hey," he added and put out his hand, "this is Black talking, color to color. We're mostly rainbow people here: Latins, Blacks and mixed bloods, except for the non-coms and officers. We're at the end of the line and colors bleed when someone has to die. But we've got some tricks of our own. Air's clear." Cooper checked the chamber of his weapon and took a deep breath. "You've been shelled before, Perez; you sweat watchful."

"Never like this," Perez answered and chambered a

round.

"Keep low and move fast. Let's check you in and set you to home."

Point, the PFC who was out front of Hartman's first patrol didn't use his given name. He answered only to Point. He was on his third tour of combat and once earned a battlefield promotion, he told Hartman.

Hartman thought Point was grandstanding, calling attention to himself to seem important. Giving Hartman the bullet and the pep talk on the first patrol was like barrack's jiving. He checked with the other troops. Point had lost his stripes for telling a shavetail to fuck himself. Point wasn't taking out a patrol until jets were called to napalm the brush. The second lieutenant, a college grad and NROTC, wrote Point up and took out the squad himself. His bars were gleaming on his collar; a sniper shot him through the neck.

Hartman asked Point why he kept coming back for more. "The States or combat, it's all the same. Except that back in the world, people want the killing camouflaged."

Point talked like that. Jerky. Hard to follow. He could not sit still for long and there were times when he spelled other soldiers on patrol—always on the point.

The other soldiers told Hartman to keep clear of Point. He's crazy and he'll get you killed.

Point was crazy but he didn't jive. The other troops seemed like they had something to hide. When he asked them about Sergeant Dibbs all they would say was that he had a name for miles around.

Point hooted when Hartman repeated what they said. "Ask them about the combat pinwheel," he told Hartman.

"Fucking Point," a man cursed at Hartman's question. "Dibbs will waste him some day for spouting off."

"I speak my mind," Point told Hartman. "What can happen? I know I'm MIA. The others are afraid to talk because they think home is still there." Point took a grenade from his belt and hefted the weight. "Dibbs knows. He'd like to handcuff me like a prisoner and throw me from a chopper."

Point was jumpy the whole day. That night on watch he gave Hartman a small black box. In the light from a flare, he showed Hartman a button and waved off questions. When darkness closed in again, Point scanned the perimeter through infrared binoculars. "Now," he whispered. Hartman pressed the button and a claymore mine exploded outside the wire: shrapnel hissed overhead with the concussion.

Someone was moaning in the dark.

"Death by remote control," Point whooped.

Point thrust a sniper rifle with a night scope at Hartman. "Shoot or listen," he said over the sound.

"You bastard," Hartman cursed and took the rifle.

2

At 0800, the entire camp was mustered at the first formation. With the full sun, the troops matched themselves against the preceding night and sensed their odds had diminished. Seized by fear, they took heart because of their numbers. Each man matched himself against the others, friends and enemies, and saw them sacrificed while he survived. And trying not to betray their bad faith, they lined up quietly.

After the section leaders had reported, Talbot put the men at rest. He watched them stand dejectedly in their own worlds. As he looked across the ranks, he was filled with disgust.

"Listen," he lashed out at them. "We don't have time for fucking games. All of you know that Delta was hit last night. You know what that means for us. You stand there looking like a bunch of raw recruits who realize finally that they're going to fight a war. Well, you're here for combat. Get it through your heads that the gooks outside that wire want you dead. One close attack and a few hours sleep and all of you are calculating if you have time to write home to mother. If slants could be killed by thinking about them, I would have already won this war. If each of you worries about his own ass, then every one is covered. So worry about your own skin and don't confuse yourselves by thinking about things that just don't matter."

Talbot stopped his harangue and the group stirred slowly back to life. Each man found the perimeter enough reason to rejoin the others and together they felt the camaraderie of the wire. Allegiance is uneasy when interests differ. But if a company of rifles is the best odds you can get, stay in the middle and hunker down. Men shifted from one leg to the other uncomfortably, and a hum of voices rose from the group. And Talbot, who saw the change in his subordinates, felt that he

drick shared their resentment. He did his best to ignore the tension. He felt like Talbot's goon in a position of leadership.

"Orozco and Taylor, check out one machine gun each. Take one man with you to handle the ammunition. Set up stations in towers twelve and fourteen to cover the men outside the wire. Put belts in the weapons and make sure they are clear and ready to fire. Keep your hands away from the triggers. We're all tired and jumpy. Talbot says he can't get replacements. They need real soldiers up north. The machine guns are just a precaution. The sun is full."

Orozco and Taylor nodded, signaled to the men they had chosen, then they broke ranks and walked toward the armory.

"I need five volunteers," Hendrick declared.

The men looked at one another, but no one came forward. "Neither first nor last and never volunteer," someone shouted from the back ranks.

"Smart thinking," Hendrick replied. "But I need five men to stay back with Ashby's group while the rest of us scout the ravine."

"Hell, I volunteer," shot back the voice in the rear. The rest of the hands went up quickly.

"Not you," Hendrick said to the voice. "I need smart men out on patrol with me." He selected the five men from the front of the assembled watch. "All of you fall out and get your full gear, including five magazines and grenades per man."

"Flak vests?" the voice asked once more.

"Full gear," Hendrick repeated.

"Shit. Why vests to stand around?" one of the men in the front ranks bitched.

"Shut up," a man behind him said. "You rather hack weeds for a day?"

"Fuck no," the voice grumbled. "This is Saturday."

A raucous laugh split the air. "Ostrowski is counting down."

"How many left, Ostrowski?" someone inquired.

"Twenty-three, you bastards."

"Whoo-ee. Twenty-three in country."

"That man is really short. The world may not be there in twenty-three, Oz, but you just keep on counting."

The rest of the men broke into laughter.

Hendrick waited for the kidding to end. "Reassemble in fifteen minutes at the front gate. We'll march around from there. Fifteen minutes. That's 0915. O.K. Fall out."

The men broke formation and started back to their huts, with their banter trailing back. "Twenty-three. Shit, he's short. I've got a hundred and forty-seven." Again someone laughed. This time the laughter struck a hollow chord and was noise.

Hendrick felt like a stooge. The patrol would be outside the wire in plain sight. Being a house nigger could get him killed. The sun was already slashing down and it had burnt off the morning's coolness. They would be moving into the light, blinded silhouettes against the glare.

Hendrick had begun to devise a plan for scouting the ravine by the time he reached the hut. The hootch was beginning to heat up. He checked his canteens and screwed the caps down tightly. As he twisted together the metal flanges of his utility belt around his waist, he heard boots moving up the steps. Priest burst into the hut, his face contorted with rage.

"That goddamn Talbot. He pulled me off Bernard's group and told me to check in with you."

"I'm taking the patrol to check out the ravine. He ordered me to take Isaacs and you along."

"That rat's ass. He's got it out for every one of us. Is Lieck coming with us?"

"No," Hendrick answered.

Priest cursed and struck a shelf that was nailed to the framing of the hut. One of the bracing struts tore free and the shelf crashed to the floor. "Lieck stays back in camp and protects his odds for survival. I'll kill that fucking Sergeant."

"In a rage," Hendrick said to Priest. "But could you frag him and say nothing ever? Talbot wants every man in this hut dead. But this patrol is not the same as going north. If we keep our heads down, we won't run into trouble. Get your gear. We meet at the front gate in ten minutes."

"This is a set-up," Priest said.

"I just imagine Talbot's out there laying in wait for us. We won't take any chances," Hendrick replied.

Unreal city where death reigned above and men went underground killing by remote control. Command Headquarters, the dispensary, any location where troops gathered was dug into the earth and piled thick with sandbags, dirt, even concrete. At this northern outpost, the incoming was unpredictable and unrelenting, Cooper told Perez hurrying him along—darting from foxhole to entrenched position. Cooper doubled back through the compound and showed Perez two key locations once more: the first-aid station and the armory. "Bullets and bandaids, Blood. Those two keep us alive. We can eat fear and shower in the dust."

Finally, Cooper took him to the living quarters. The entrance snaked into the earth and Perez knew the curve was to stop the fragments and blast from a direct hit at the mouth of the fortified hut. Smoky and ill-lit, he saw shapes.

"You know better than to bring a cracker in here, Cooper," someone said.

"This is Perez, troops, Latino and a disciplinary transfer. He almost took off a sergeant's head for naming him bad."

"*Pérez*," another voice echoed. "Coño," the shape said moving forward. "Are you 'Rican?"

"No," Perez replied. "Chicano."

"Hey, Pana, we got us a connection. Mexican-American to my New York Puerto Rican. I'm *Fernández*," he said, grasped his hand and they shook out the salute. "Vaya! Hermano, there's one bet—nothing worse can happen to us. I'll take him from here, Cooper."

Fernandez showed him to his cot and introduced him to the rest of the squad. He joked nonstop with the others who relaxed and went back to playing cards. Perez went to his cot and began unpacking his gear. Fernandez sat down at one end. "Watch yourself, Perez. They're allies but right at the edge. A wrong word, even a look gets you wasted. You're in our tent, so you'll be marked as one of us. I look like them, you don't, but remember who your friends are. The non-coms and officers are Blancos and we Trigueños and Spics are expendable. You got to follow direct orders, but remember we're just numbers. Obey orders during the day but always keep your head down. Night," Fernandez said, "is mad time and the game changes."

Perez looked at him and Fernandez met his eyes coolly. "This camp is a killing ground and no one can be trusted."

"Not even you, Carnal?"

Fernandez laughed. "Rank and power rule; all we Rainbows got is each other. You're from the streets?"

"My family lived in East Los, but we moved when I was young. You?"

"Spanish Harlem is my turf. Or was. I got to clear this place."

"How much time?"

"Coño, Pana. We don't count time here. Four months is a tour at this post, but I don't know nobody who made it that long. Only two tickets out: medevacked or bagged in plastic. The brass gave us a one-way ride. I hope you messed up that sergeant good."

"I hit him."

"Mano a mano, right? You looked him in the face and

went for his throat. Coño, we got smarter ways," Fernandez said, and patted a grenade on his utility belt. "Always carry ten magazines plus the one in your weapon. Four grenades minimum. Never stay still in the open because of the incoming and snipers. Most people get zapped because they let down their guard a moment. Too long at the shitter, an uncovered match on post. We got to stay alive and tell our brothers."

"You ordered me to report to you, Sergeant," Hartman said, as he stood at attention in front of Talbot.

"You hear all right, at least. There are a couple of things I have to cover and now is as good a time as any. I see that you put in a request to be Kirsch's driver and birddog on those so-called medical missions he makes to the villages surrounding us. You know no one else wants the job?"

"I know that, Sergeant," Hartman said, braced at attention.

"I have to order men to go with him. No one ever volunteers. The rest of the men feel it's a waste of time. No one knows who the enemy is in this hell hole. Chances are that most of the people Kirsch treats are the enemy. We've heard that those two-faced slants save the medicine that Kirsch passes out and give it to the sappers."

"I heard the others say that, Sergeant."

Talbot's eyes bore into Hartman's face. "What do you think?"

"I've seen their dead with our supplies. They could have taken medicine from our dead, from pilfered stock. I've seen our medicine on the black market . . ."

"I'm not talking about pills," Talbot cut him off. "I'm talking about Kirsch."

"I've been with Kirsch in the villages. He treats women and children."

"Kirsch treats mainly women and children because their men are in the hills lining up their rockets on us," Talbot said, his voice rising.

Hartman said nothing.

"He should question his loyalties, Hartman. You too. You've got to stand with us or the medic." Talbot waited for a reaction, but Hartman remained silent. "You know, Corporal, that Delta was hit from that village four miles away from this camp. If I had my way, I would have leveled that dung pile."

Hartman kept his face expressionless, but Talbot thought that the corporal's eyes looked at him strangely, as if he were seeing someone else.

"Their soldiers know how to force us into mistakes," Hartman finally said. "If that village is leveled, we lose anyone who sides with us. If it was in enemy hands, they would not risk attacking us from there. They could have hit Delta from other places."

"Kirsch gives those gooks too much credit," replied Talbot. "They hit us from Four-Miles because they know we couldn't retaliate. Too many of his women and kids in it. If we're hit again with rockets, that village will be incinerated. If we find anything alive, we will relocate it where those gooks can't get at us. You still want to work for Kirsch after I told you what's going on? I can cancel your request."

"No!" Hartman answered, too quick in Talbot's judgment.

"Your choice: live with it! I'm attaching you to Kirsch today. I'm even pulling you off our roster and watch list. You can carry the sea lawyer's medicines for him. Maybe you can ship over with the Navy."

Talbot's eyes locked onto Hartman's face. "What makes a man from a line company up north volunteer for duty with a medic? Quit hiding. Admit what's on your mind."

Hartman's face remained empty, except for his eyes which regarded Talbot as if Hartman were trying to make something out in the dark. "Am I dismissed, Sergeant?" the corporal asked in a level tone of voice.

"One more thing," Talbot said. "I want you to move in with Priest and Isaacs and the others. Change huts right now."

"Yes, Sergeant." Hartman did an about face and left.

I'll find you out Hartman, Talbot thought. It's just a matter of time.

"Don't be pissed," Point told Hartman. "Those sappers were cutting the wire. You kill or die."

"You set me up, Point. I don't kill wounded."

"Dibbs doesn't take prisoners, wounded or not. If they can talk, he loads them in a chopper. High up, he interrogates them and no matter what, he drops them. The combat pinwheel." Point rotated his fingers around each other, whistled like incoming and went, "whap."

"You know why this war is lost?" Point asked, throwing Hartman off balance. "The enemy knows about Dibbs. In a firefight, when wounded, they pull the pin on a grenade and lay down on the weapon. Whoever moves them gets blown up. If Dibbs takes them alive, and drops them at altitude, they don't scream—don't give him satisfaction . . ."

"Pull some sick stunt like that again, Point, and I'll push the button on you," Hartman told him.

"See," Point said, and his eyes glittered. "It was good I made you off them. Now you understand. Home ends at the wire, and no one goes back. States or combat—nothing's real except the killing. The enemy has a cause. We have technology. Got to kill them all."

Hartman was so tired he fell asleep after dark, even with

Point on the loose.

Rotting burlap and damp earth—a musty, sweaty odor permeated the underground bunker. Thinking was a reptile's sense of smell. Tiered sandbags heaved in sync with the blasts and concussion from mortar, rocket and howitzer. In the emplacement, the dust from the close calls scoured his lungs.

Close, Perez' legs jerked in spasms and dirt clods tattooed the plywood floor. Again—timbers rattling and the wheezy soil. He forced the air out of his lungs in deep breaths so that he would not make a sound. Maria, back home you said my silence was killing me and that I was burying myself in books. Outside, death shrieked like *la llorona*, the woman of legend who wailed for her lost children.

"Why can't you admit that you're Mexican?" she had asked at college. Maria made Perez question his identity.

"I have lived in the United States all my life. I am not a citizen of Mexico. But I know I'm not an Anglo," he answered her and held out his arm next to hers. His compañera challenged his thinking about who he was.

Perez felt the gritty dust on his arms from the incoming and told himself, I am neither Mexican nor Anglo, neither Catholic nor Protestant, neither Spaniard nor Indian. I am as if suspended between different worlds, between the blast and aftershock, between one shell and the following round.

"Who are your people?" she once flared as they struggled to understand one another at the beginning of their relationship. "Don't talk in abstractions. Forget Western philosophy and the isolated self. No one lives solo. You're *sangre* and *hueso*, blood and bone, and you live only with people who are like you."

Mestizo-mestizaje: he was the mix of Spanish conquistador and Mesoamerican Indian—neither the one nor the other but a synthesis he had to create. Not Hispanic, as if Europe were better. Not Mexican-American, which had the facile inflection of the Melting Pot. Give me your tired . . . a new people. White is American. He was Chicano. Stay alive. His name was the point in the shrill incoming.

Chicanos marched on city hall during Perez' junior year to protest against the politicians who gerrymandered communities. Maria challenged him to act. Together, they joined with other university students who stormed the Board of Education and shouted down Dick and Jane—the White-way right-way teachers. They demanded textbooks that allowed children to learn about their history and culture in the Spanish language they used in their homes and which made them citizens of a hemisphere.

Another group picketed finance companies that red-lined the barrios. The wagons were drawn in a circle around the Indians. Perez watched his compatriots. Years of failed promises were over.

"Have you always known who you are?" he asked her once in baffled rage. He had not found answers in books.

She talked about her migrant background and working in the fields, about small rural towns and her traditional Catholic upbringing. Being Chicana didn't fit what sociologists know.

"Our backgrounds are unique," Maria agreed with Perez. "We have to stand for ourselves."

"I learned two lessons from my background: hard work and silence." Finally, Perez could say I to her. "My parents didn't have time. Even as kids, their hands were calloused. They never talked much about roots or how they saw the world. Long hours and low wages meant a home and education, and they watched their children grow without the sense of being buried alive on the bottom."

She hugged him close with surprising strength. He was

angry for feeling like a sell-out, angry with his parents for their narrowed lives.

After meeting Talbot, Perez understood why he learned to keep silent. Once he let himself feel, Perez could shoot to kill.

Talbot. Spic, half-breed, dumb Mexican—constant insults and contempt. Perez' fist in that sergeant's sneering face. The blow was payment for his father. The ditch at work caved in and left him in a coma for two days. Three vertebrae fractured when the earthen wall at the construction site collapsed. He would walk but never be the same.

His father's face was ashen in the glaring hospital light. Bruised, scraped and flecked with crusty blood—he drifted in and out of consciousness and spoke both in English and Spanish. Perez' father rarely spoke Spanish, because English got hired. But because of Maria, Perez was able to understand. "Trabajo," his father said, "estoy listo." Or he would reach for a pocket and declare, "I have my papers; I'm not illegal." The nurses had to restrain him so that he would not tear out his tubing.

Even injured, his father was trying to make a home. A country he had helped build for fifty years wanted papers.

When the bombardment slackened and Fernandez checked the bunker with a battle lamp, he found Perez beating his fists against rotting sacks.

Two helicopters clattered over the dispensary and veered off toward the mountains. As they turned, their camouflaged bodies blended with the dark heights and disappeared. Only the rotors remained visible, blurs of light. Even these traces sometimes vanished, like paired images that cancel each other out.

Kirsch swept and mopped the dispensary with disinfectant. The stocks of new supplies and medicine were double checked, sorted and stored. There was nothing left to do except wait for sick-call. Kirsch went to his makeshift desk and chose a pencil from a number he kept sharpened. A lined regulation tablet was almost full of entries: the worn pages were held together by a clipboard. Sometimes pages wrote themselves. Whose hand? Kirsch wondered. Unsent letters or memos: to whomever this concerns.

In a rear-guard camp during a guerilla war, day-to-day life becomes ennui broken by sudden terror. Everything comes down to one thought, surviving a tour of duty. Troops greet each other with a constant refrain: only two hundred, only eighty-three, only so many more days to go. "I'm getting short, I'll be home soon." There is nothing to discuss except an escape. Hours measure nothing: light and dark are two sides of waiting. Time leaches any thoughts except returning home.

"We soldiers move from day to night over and again, chanting our litanies of escape." Talking to yourself again, Kirsch. The medic looked around the dispensary uneasily.

Time contracts to boredom and fear. Each one of the men I know, Priest, Isaacs, even Lieck, deals with them in his own way. After a matter of months even these constants blur. Perhaps to survive, soldiers go numb. Fear becomes a fatalistic sort of joking about death. What do you call your top sergeant in civilian clothes? The Grim Reaper. Terror is a paralysis of the spirit. The attack we fear will surely come. We have not been rocketed or mortared in months. No sense of relief because our number is up.

If we are lucky, no one will be killed, just maimed or medevacked. Terror is like dying. Almost better to accept the belief that if your number is up, then it's up. Letting fate be a death sentence stops the wheels. For every day in garrison spared from attack, there is a night. The dark belongs to the unseen enemy who is a master of surprise. At war how can a man be bored? Tedious routine makes life contract. If a soldier repeats useless tasks all day long, time becomes like the heat. Even the threat of death can be diminished by repetition.

Modern technology refashioned into tools of war is inescapable. Our trucks are weapons of transportation. Assembly line new, these vehicles are more than freight carriers. Machine guns are welded onto their cabs and boxes of belted ammunition are bolted into place beside the guns. The devastating efficiency of our machines makes itself part of the battlefield.

The country spews out goods that are shipped to this war. We march and counter-march, leaving our wreckage strewn about the countryside. The factories produce day and night. Everyone has work. The armies are resupplied and the destruction continues. Destruction and production seem the same.

Technology takes war out of the trenches, but does not make us human. The electricity in our plain but efficient dwellings, the water we pipe in from reservoirs in the foothills make dying hideous and absurd. Asleep in our plywood huts, or as we shave with blades honed to surgical sharpness, we can die. For all our so-called technological advances, we can die as did those who bludgeoned each other to death with rough clubs. We kill at a distance with the concussion from rockets or artillery, disembowel men with the shrapnel from sophisticated mines or mortars.

If we lived in trenches with no light or running water, then there might be less contradiction between our skills and what use we make of our hands. In this encampment ringed with barbed wire, the disparity between the best of our hopes and guerilla warfare is too obvious. Splitters of the atom, we cannot escape the oldest of evils.

Hartman heard the receding chop of two helicopters as he crossed Talbot's camp to the dispensary. His boots crushed into the powdered earth and it exploded into clouds of dust around his footprints. Behind him, the dust hung in the air like tracks of haze. As he walked, he rubbed the film of sweat and dust from his palms. He knocked at the rear door of the dispensary. Kirsch responded and he went inside. The corpsman was at his desk and did not look up. The medic was staring at a piece of paper, not really seeing anything. He did that often. Hartman rapped on the plywood partition that divided the room and called Kirsch's name. Kirsch recovered quickly.

"I've been assigned to you," Hartman told him.

"Talbot asked if I needed help. He said something about a reassignment. I didn't think he was serious. I can use you."

"Talbot is always Talbot," Hartman said. "He just ordered a patrol outside the wire."

Kirsch stood up. "When?"

"At muster," replied Hartman.

"He makes sure that I go out with any patrol. If Priest were in charge, I would understand what he's doing."

"Priest and Isaacs are scouting with Hendrick," Hartman added.

"Another set-up. Do I have time to catch them?" Kirsch asked while he started gathering his gear.

"The patrol was already forming at the main gate. They must be outside the wire already."

"That bastard," Kirsch said, as he put down his medical pack and went to the rear door of the hut. "He timed it perfect."

Talbot put men on patrol and counted on mines or booby traps. Sergeant Dibbs shot troops in the back. Hartman assumed that Point was invulnerable. "I just don't give a fuck," Point always told him and that curse became his charm. The enemy could not kill him, even though he was always on the point. Trust nobody. Anyone can be the enemy. Yet Point never figured Dibbs would shoot him in the back.

There was no way to prove that Dibbs shot Point. Anyone could see that Point was killed by a heavy charge, high velocity 7.62mm bullet from a sniper rifle. Since it was dark, the rifle had to have a night scope. But the weapon could have been captured from U.S. troops in battle or stolen. Hartman could not say.

The patrol brought Point back quick and the medic did everything he could. But the bullet caught him in the neck where the flak vest didn't cover. It would have probably killed Point through the vest, anyway.

Hartman helped bag Point's remains and felt strange, as if he were split up. He was helping the corpsman and yet somewhere else watching them zip up the body bag.

Dibbs had ordered Point's patrol out with artillery cover. Everyone in the camp was underground, in case of stray rounds. No one would pay attention to a single round of fire from a sniper rifle and it was dark. Point was hit close to the wire, even before the patrol was in the brush. Sergeant Dibbs sent for Hartman while the weight of the body bag and the scraping sounds were there. Dibbs bellowed at Hartman that he better toe the mark now that Point was dead.

"That smart ass got his ticket punched. Don't forget who's in command."

Hartman had never looked close at Dibbs. Across from him in the bunker under an incandescent bulb, Dibbs had the bloodless waxy look of Point. Then the lips cracked in half-smile, half-scowl, catching Hartman back at the body bag.

"You got it, Hartman? I put out the orders. There ain't no place left to hide."

Why tell me this? Hartman thought. I never hid behind Point. He just stood between me and you, between you and the men. Right then something went clear, like when he focused on the wounded sappers through the sniper scope.

Hartman took out a handkerchief, wiped his face and used the cover to search the space. In a corner away from the light was a sniper rifle with a night scope. The weapon was in the shadows, yet in plain sight. Dibbs wouldn't be stupid and leave a murder weapon in the open.

And Hartman thought, why not? Who is there to fear, now that Point is dead? You're telling me to say nothing, keep in line or else, Hartman realized. Death by remote control. Wasn't that what Point always said?

On one side was Point. On the other was Dibbs. Even shot in the back, Point was right again. Fight a guerilla war and everyone's the enemy.

Hartman put away the cloth and looked at Dibbs once more.

"You got it, Marine?" Dibbs shouted at him.

"Aye, aye, Sir," Hartman shouted back and left. I'm starting to understand this war. Kill and don't give a fuck.

Point was dead and Dibbs would not let any grunt in the outfit forget. With him out of the way, Dibbs started riding the troops, as if he had to protect his command. More patrols, longer watches and Dibbs was watching Hartman all the while.

Since Hartman and Point were watchmates, Sergeant Dibbs must have figured Hartman had a score to settle because of Point's murder. Yet Point was not a friend whose killing demanded revenge. He had been a dangerous ally who spoke his mind, no matter what, because he was not scared of dying and did not believe in home.

Point had forced Hartman to finish two sappers that Point had blown up with a claymore mine. Point set up the explosive device on patrol and booby-trapped it twice. One sapper cut the main trip-wire and neutralized one of the traps. He must have figured the mine was safe and picked it up because the upper torso was in shreds.

No one felt they had to pay Dibbs back. But when Dibbs

started getting them killed on extra patrols at night and put Hartman in charge of harvesting bodies from the wire, things changed. Any time the enemy charged the perimeter, Hartman was ordered out at daybreak to pluck dead gooks snared by barbed wire. Sometimes they were shot up so bad, they came apart in chunks. Sometimes not. There was an element of chance. Dibbs ordered Hartman outside the wire to clear the bodies always at daybreak. A routine makes you vulnerable because someone can predict where to fire. Hartman realized that when Dibbs took out Point, he became unfinished business. Hartman went out with the grave detail, eyes peeled, no slack in the trigger. Any noise from the brush and they would start jamming, and then the grunts in the camp would start shooting like someone yelled madfire, and Dibbs was out there figuring who's next?

The dead ripened overnight, so that the faces were bloated and the taut skin was blanched and dull by daybreak. Often they looked like Point, and Hartman wondered what would Point say? "I just don't give a fuck. It's all the same."

Got to be regular—the bodies and first light coming like the dead were brooding over the desolation. And Hartman started feeling as if he were not there when he was plucking them. The touch of the corpses was real—spongy like the flesh was full of maggots underneath. But Hartman was off watching to the side. That split-up sense of who he was almost got him killed.

The body came off the wire and grabbed him by the throat, choking him, and Hartman fell back and a knee got him in the plexus. The hands were cutting off his air. Pain from the blow gagged him. He braced his hands against the ground and tried to roll his attacker off. The grip held. A rock was there and he bashed the head above him. Blood sprayed and Hartman struck again as he was blacking out. The hands loosened and as Hartman sucked in air, someone fired close and the attacker's head exploded. Hartman choked on tissue and blood.

"Where are you hit?" someone shouted and tore open his shirt, as if he had a chest wound.

Hartman vomited and tried to breathe. When he got enough air, he started to laugh. "See," he said and wiped the gore from his face. "Death by remote control."

"You almost bought it, mother-fuck."

"Naw. They can't touch me now," he said, coughing from the laughter. "I'm MIA."

The first thing he saw when he got back was the cigar box that Point had used to keep his things. He held out the box to the ones who helped him, saying, "I put in fifty for Dibbs. Who else is aboard?"

Some put up money without a word. Others looked strange.

And Hartman laughed at the expressions and felt a surge of elation. "This is for ghosts. We'll take care of business the American way." They must have understood, because no one refused money.

The back of his uniform under the fragment vest was soaked with sweat when Hendrick caught sight of the patrol grouped in an open area near the main gate. He lifted the vest up and off his neck and settled it lower on his spine feeling the weight press in against the bone. Each step jolted the steel helmet on his head. Rather than fasten it, Hendrick straightened the pot from time to time, wanting not to look like a poster soldier rushing to do battle.

A few of the men had found sparse patches of dried weeds around the sentry's station and they stayed put. "You're late," one of them called out to Hendrick.

"I was checking with the towers and Ashby's bunch.

Come on, get on your feet. The sooner we get this over, the better."

The men automatically lined up in three ranks, and edged and sidled until they were aligned with each other.

"Everyone has their magazines and canteens?" Hendrick questioned, and no one spoke up. "The five of you I chose for guard detail will wait for Ashby right here. We'll check your area and then move to the ravine. The patrol won't be searching more than a few miles from the camp. Those of you coming with me, listen carefully. We'll advance in a skirmish line through the low brush near the perimeter, check the wire, form a column at the ravine, and then we'll play it by ear. Check the magazines in your weapons, chamber a round and keep the safety on until we get into the brush. I don't want us shooting each other."

"All right, all right, let's go," Ostrowski muttered.

Hendrick fastened his chin strap and inserted a magazine into his rifle. "O.K.," Hendrick said. "Column of files from the right, move out after me."

Hendrick led the men onto the dirt road, feeling the pinch of the strap against his chin. The patrol filed along the road until the group was in line with the furthest curve of the wire. Hendrick stopped and searched the brush between the road and the wire. He saw nothing suspicious, and so he stepped over a graded rill of earth at the margin of the road and made his way into the undergrowth. He waved men to his right and left and they skirmished through the dry vegetation looking for tracks.

The dry brush snapped off loudly under his feet, and branches dug into his legs. Hendrick heard someone cursing to his left. When he looked down, he saw the blousing of his trousers covered with large, yellow burrs, rimmed in red. A drop of sweat rolled down his forehead toward his right eye. He tried to wipe the wetness away with the cuff of his shirt. He forgot his bulky helmet and wiped the wet into the eye, feeling the sudden salt sting and the rush of tears. He stopped, put the wire at his back and rubbed the eye until it eased. Then Hendrick resumed his search.

The march along the cleared ground was quick. The charred ends of the fired undergrowth gave off the hot trace smell of kerosene. Further on, the open area was a red ochre scar that would remain barren until the rains came.

Hendrick pictured the ravine cutting in diagonally on the camp and looked ahead to where he thought the gash curved and ran its course parallel to the wire. Taylor pointed from the tower, his finger snaking in a curve and then moving back to lock in place. Ashby would start cutting back the brush where the ravine was closest to the coils of barbed steel. Hendrick led the men there.

"Take a blow," Hendrick said, after the patrol reached their first objective. He squatted down on the ground, panting and hot. He jerked at his helmet strap and opened his mouth to breathe. Hendrick ignored the oily smell, and shielded his eyes. The glare of the sun was sharp and pain grated his right eye. He blinked and focused his attention on a clump of brush.

"Son of a bitching heat," Ostrowski cursed. He picked angrily at the burrs clinging to his boot laces and threw them at the ravine. "Let's get this goddamn circus on the road."

"All right," Hendrick said. He braced himself with his rifle and stood up.

Suddenly, there was a loud rustling in the brush. Hendrick crouched down quickly and released the safety with a flick of his right hand.

"What was that?" Ostrowski asked and his voice cracked.

"I thought I saw a snake," one of the men said. "I threw a rock, that's all."

Ostrowski was prone on the earth with his rifle to his shoulder. He looked over at the man who had thrown the rock. "Do that again and I'll kick your fucking head in."

"All right, let's go," Hendrick ordered, breaking the tension before it built more. "Everyone on your feet. Move along the wire again and check it."

Hendrick walked toward the ravine and the thick cover of vegetation. Ashby's group would be working here. Three men from the guard detail would stand down in front and there would be one man on either flank. The patrol would be in the ravine. He had given careful instructions that no one was to fire . . .

"Oh, Christ, not now."

Hendrick spun around, transfixed by the voice. The glaring light made everything ominous. His motion seemed slow as if imminent disaster had stopped time.

"The wire's cut," Ostrowski yelled. "They cut the wire."

After the discovery that the barbed wire at the perimeter had been breached under cover of darkness, the men left back at Talbot's camp worked at an unrelenting pace. They concentrated on their jobs and only when the heat got to them did they take a break. Locked into their tasks, each soldier came to the panicked moment when he realized there was no escape. A grunt would stop working and look out beyond the wire, and feel a gritty uniform cling to sweaty skin. The blasting heat was oppressive. What use was the work? Would a few more trenches keep them alive? A few more rows of sandbags make a difference?

Wills went slack and the men abandoned hope. They looked at the other troops working as if it mattered. Fools. How did you fight an enemy no one could see?

But Delta had been hit and only one KIA—in his bunk by a direct hit from a mortar. If the patrol wasn't hit, the whole camp would know what was ahead. Each man looked at the others and took their silent despair as a sign of determination. Each man knew what to expect and each man vowed not to be careless. How many of the dead were fools who let down their guard or took a chance?

———————

"*Oye, hermano*, you'll die quick if you lose your head." Fernandez offered Perez his canteen. Perez' hands were scraped and bleeding from the bags.

The small circle of men murmured their assent. In the light from the battlelamp, their faces gleamed eerily.

"The suckers in charge have slick ways to beat you down," Johnson said and put his hand on Perez' shoulder. "At least the incoming is straight up. The Man will grease you on the hottest point of the perimeter. He'll work your ass the whole day, then nail you to the night roster. He wants you to make a mistake and check in your piece. His conscience is White and you're bagged meat.

"Remember what that fucking Slater tried to do to us?" Fernandez asked the group. "He told Cooper that I was bad-mouthing Blacks. Then he turned around and told me that the Blacks were reaming Mestizos. Cooper and I talked and found out his downside ride."

"That redneck took a ride," Johnson burst out. "Why should we Rainbows fight among ourselves and do the Man's work for him? Color is not the game. Power and money bleed everyone."

"Slater wound up in pieces," Fernandez said. "He went to take a shit and turned up *mierda*. Zapped in private. The Board of Inquiry determined that he was wasted by a grenade. From where—who knows?"

"That gung-ho bastard cost Uribe his life. Slater put him on every patrol, put him on the point and got him killed. Uribe was a Tex-Mex with soul," Johnson continued.

"He was macho," Fernandez declared. "And Slater nailed him. If he wanted off the point, the cracker told him to pick someone from our hootch to go for him. So Uribe told Slater 'I know the enemy.' "

"Yeah," Johnson agreed. "We were just niggers minding our own business back home. The Man reached out and grabbed us by the throat. I wasn't concerned about nothing—just getting by. After this war I ain't going back.

The shelling had lifted but everyone waited in case of madfire.

"Hold your fire," Hendrick yelled at the patrol. He had led them to a hilltop where they were checking out the farmers in the paddies and staying hidden. "Who started firing?"

Ostrowski muttered, "All them yellow bastards are the enemy. They cut the fucking wire."

"They're growing rice," Hendrick told him.

"Now. But after dark, they hit us."

"Take five. Jesus!" Hendrick said and nothing else. This war put life back home up front. White soldiers called the local people gooks, slant-eyes, yellow meat, yaller niggers. The color of skin fixed the enemy. Back home Hendrick knew that color can get you killed if you walk the wrong side of the street. Find some friendly faces and get ethnic, because all you have is each other.

Hendrick looked at Isaacs and was relieved that no one in the paddies was hit. If only Isaacs could think with his skin and not feel so much.

Rebo Tufoy, his friend back home, would take to Isaacs. Isaacs was Gospel, although he was white. Like Rebo, he was looking for a quiet place, only Isaacs thought that God abandoned him and Rebo wasn't sure He was there.

Hendrick knew who his people were, but he was not staying in the ghetto. In high school, he worked serious. Nothing but elbows flying from hauling and toting. No matter that most of his friends, even the smart ones, dropped out. He started putting away money from his job after school and his parents were saving all they could. Cooking burgers for shit wages convinced him to get out. He walked fifteen blocks home rather than ride the bus and let people look down their noses at him. Grease was all over him as was the odor of cooking. The job sucked, but that's how he met Rebo.

Some new tablewipe tried to make a customer leave because he was just sitting over a book drinking coffee, Hendrick recalled. "Hey, Blood, got to live together," the man told the help. "Just don't go pushing on me." The stupid fool grabbed Rebo by the arm and told him, ain't no library. Hendrick stepped in, told the new hire he was wanted in the back and offered more coffee. The dude at the table was on his feet and just said, "don't jive. Let me be." Hendrick tried to figure something smooth, pointed to a contest ad for a tropic vacation and said, "no, man. Aloha spirit," and refilled his cup.

Rebo Tufoy was a disabled vet who was alive because of a Samoan brother Rebo had buried in Hawaii. Rebo made up a new name for himself because it sounded like his friend. Anything Hawaiian and Rebo was on your side. Hendrick was lucky with friends. After graduation, he wondered what to do. Rebo told him to work two jobs, use one to live and save the money from the other for college. "Got to live on the fly, if you want out of the streets."

Rebo was Gospel, sang the old music in a choir. Hendrick went along once. "Like the music—can't go the words, Rebo."

"Sometimes I'm singing and the feeling's there," he told Hendrick. "Gospel helps me sleep."

"Say?" Hendrick replied.

"Everybody needs rest. Like sanctuary—somewhere peaceful in the noise."

"Not yet," Hendrick told him. "I'm still here."

It was Rebo who was sanctuary when the draft notice came. Rebo who stayed with him not saying much, just being right there. Isaacs was torn up by war. Now it was Hendrick's turn.

When the shock of the letter wore down, and Hendrick started asking, "What do I do?", Rebo responded, "What matters?"

"I want to live where the streets don't bring me down. I want to cruise without watching the mirror."

Rebo took him to talk to his grandfather, a veteran of WWII. "White folk called that one a good war. They segregated us and left us in the rear. Today you all get to die equal some place I never heard. Lemme tell you straight—I can't even guess what we're fighting for. Maybe they need an enemy. Better yellow folk than us."

"You heard?" Rebo asked him.

"Listen, dude. You were in uniform, so why the jiving?" Rebo gave him a few bars of something about watchtowers and the night.

Then the brothers on the street got the word and came around.

"You going to war and be their nigger?" they asked Hendrick.

"They need your black ass to test their bombs: Frosty's answer to unemployment."

"Hey, Clem. Why you want to bleed for Superman?"

Rebo didn't say a word. He let Hendrick do the talking.

"Stay here," the brothers told Hendrick. "You can lay low and they'll never find you."

"Listen. This is your turf and I ain't badmouthing. But shit. I feel like I'm buried alive."

"This turf is it, man. These streets is all there is."

And Hendrick didn't want to push it, so he just said to himself, a lot of you right here will be dead from booze and dope and guns. Rag on me about combat?

Instead, Hendrick joked, "If I go north to Canada, will I stick out in the snow?"

Fight or run. He had to decide. Finally he came right out and asked Rebo what he should do. And Rebo told him, "I'm a vet and don't give advice. Everybody does the wire in their way."

"Shit, Rebo. Don't come on like John Wayne. Talk to me."

"O.K. I tell you this. The wire is already out there, man, only you don't see it. Live to the perimeter. Don't take a step without it being worth dying for."

"What?" Hendrick said. "You off somewhere?"

"One more time," Rebo Tufoy told him. "Ordinary life is combat in disguise. The killing is out of sight. That draft letter makes it plain. Don't do nothing without figuring if it's worth the dying. That's Rebo's line on the perimeter."

"I get your meaning, Rebo. In uniform I might be wasted. Back in the streets I'm dead for sure. If I survive this tour, I can go to college on VA, just like you." Rebo was studying English and writing a book on the war.

Hendrick looked at the farmers who were starting back to work in the paddies. "You got your war. I got mine. We're both betting against the house. Just don't come through the wire and make me waste you."

When the patrol saw the farmers in the rice fields, Isaacs knew what would happen before the shooting started. He wanted to serve, to be of use, not shoot civilians. Isaacs would have registered as a conscientious objector if he had known about war. He thought he could defend the flag, even though he had never even been to a funeral. Once he put on a uniform, there was no going back. Even Kirsch, the medic, said that he would draw his .45 if the perimeter were overrun. He was a corpsman, yet scourged by wire too.

Once, Isaacs believed that God was in the world and Satan was outside trying to destroy the good. The perimeter was blasphemy. Old beliefs eroded with each patrol, with every watch. No dogma lasted in the flares.

The gunfire, the villagers, Hendrick yelling at the men to stop firing—those were real. But when Isaacs looked around, everything seemed to waver as if from heat. There were no bodies this time, just frightened people in the muck. Maybe not tonight nor tomorrow nor the day or night after that—but the time was close. He felt doomed. Pray and the words echoed in a void. Once he shot to kill, he could never hope to be whole. God was too far away.

Sarah could not understand. Although she loved him, she was in another world. Even when they last touched, part of him was at the wire. "Try to forget," she said. Yet he could not. Even as he held her close, he thought God has withdrawn behind a perimeter. How can I believe in us when I feel empty and alone?

———

Talbot slapped a fist into his palm and swiveled his chair around so that he faced Fortecca. "What do you mean an army couldn't get through the wire? You spliced together the cut strands and laid down new coils: do you think that makes this camp secure? Tell me, Fortecca, how could those yellow wizards cut the wire in the first place and not be seen? There are posts circling this camp and not one reported anything. And now you're telling me a few strands of wire will make a difference. The enemy might as well march through the front gate, for all the good the wire will do us."

Fortecca was beaten down and his lips congealed into a twisted grin. "I know that the gooks got to us clean," he said trying to salvage some of his self-respect. "But I thought, now that we know what to expect, that we'll be ready for them."

"You thought! I'm surrounded by incompetents who do nothing but think. I would rather have morons who can see and who can follow orders."

Fortecca looked at Talbot and his grin disappeared. Bernard put down his eyes and stared at the floor.

"And you, Bernard," Talbot said. "Do you have anything to add?"

"Nothing, Sergeant," responded Bernard.

"The trenches are finished?" Talbot inquired.

"Yes." Bernard looked over at Fortecca. "The trenches are deep enough for graves."

"There's room for you then, Bernard," Talbot told him. "Keep your cap on straight and don't try me, unless you want to travel. You're dismissed, both of you. Send in Hendrick."

In his office, Talbot reigned with complete self-assurance. His authority was clear and his relationships with both the officers and the enlisted men was defined by his rank. This one corner of the camp was the only place Talbot allowed himself to relax. One swivel chair; an old gray desk, cleared and well-dusted; a tiered, regulation issued desk file, block printed for "OUTGOING," "INCOMING," and those papers consigned to "HOLD"; one heavy mug with a broken handle for pencils and pens; an empty howitzer casing filled with sand that served as an ashtray; one shelf above and behind the desk that was braced up by two-by-fours and which held military manuals. Of necessity, there was a rough bench braced against and backed by a plywood wall. Outside his office, there were myriad exigencies of rank that might confuse anyone. Inside Talbot's office, the man and his surroundings so defined each other, that they constituted his limits and his freedom.

At his desk, Talbot would plan his actions and sort his men. After a succession of offices and desks, Talbot knew his own mind. He was an individual who had come to know his prejudices in long, tedious years when he was left to himself. In his office, Talbot would not allow himself to be called into question.

Hendrick knocked and entered the office, wiping the sweat from his face with his folded cap. Talbot took out a map from a desk drawer and unrolled it on the desk top. Motioning for Hendrick to move closer, he weighted the curling ends of the thick paper under two dome-shaped pieces of transparent glass with the insignia of the Corps glued to their flat surfaces.

Talbot traced a finger along the map. "The ravine is here. How far did you search?"

"We followed it south until it bottomed out at Hill 302," Hendrick indicated. "Three men searched through it as we went south. They cut their way through the brush where it was thick. The rest of the patrol skirmished on both sides of the ravine and looked for signs.

"We climbed Hill 302 and watched the area. No one saw movement, no smoke or dust. We returned north following the ravine, searching as we had done going south. We went past our camp and left the ravine to scout the village."

"What about the village?" inquired Talbot.

"We worked behind a small hill and watched it from concealment. Nothing looked suspicious. Some of the patrol worked around behind it without giving themselves away. The rest of us moved down and cordoned the village off. We checked I.D. cards and regrouped. No one tried to get away from us."

"That was a good patrol," Talbot said abruptly. He rolled up the map and put it away. "I don't have a fucking thing more to go on than when the patrol left. Still," he said reflectively, "that was a good job." He looked at Hendrick keenly and nodded to himself. "We are two sides of the same coin, you and I. We do what we have to and don't make excuses."

Talbot leaned back in his chair. "You know how to deal with men in authority. You keep your head and you know when to keep quiet."

Hendrick was thrown off balance by Talbot's behavior. Suddenly, he was aware of the taste of dust in his mouth and he felt the fine particles of earth like a membrane against his face.

"You're a good scout," and Talbot smiled in his thin, starved way. "You're cut out to be a Marine. You know, once I heard my brother say the world will not end in fire. Instead of incinerating itself, the universe will drift apart in all directions, run out of juice, and freeze into a dead bloc of space. That was the only thing he ever said that makes sense to me. A man has to marshall his energy or he runs down. He must discipline himself, hold to a course of action, prove himself by his own effort. I owe allegiance to my country and the flag." Talbot gripped the arms of his chair. "I prove our tradition right by keeping our country on top of the world. I corroborate my beliefs by my actions. The issues and questions that word-merchants argue over, I leave to their ilk. Let them argue over right or truth until the world freezes over."

Talbot looked intently at Hendrick, observing his every reaction. "Your face is an open book, Hendrick. Everything you think is written on your face."

"What do you want, Talbot?" Hendrick finally said.

"Sergeant!" Talbot snapped. "Don't ever forget that." The room closed in. "I want nothing, Hendrick, except to tell you that you are too valuable a man to waste. But I will not give any man slack. Once committed to a cause, a soldier does not waver. You sacrifice the effort that gives purpose to your life; if you permit questions or doubts, you undermine the disciplined force that is your only alternative. To doubt your own cause is indecision; compassion for the enemy is weakness. I will not be challenged and I want no slackers. I have no time to slap wrists. Tell the others not to cross me, keep their mouths shut and learn from you. There won't be any trouble then."

Hendrick was ordered from the office and he was too exhausted to consider all that Talbot had said. When the patrol had returned to the camp, he and the other men had taken a fifteen-minute break. They watched the men in the other work parties finishing the last tasks outside the wire. The air was thick with dust because of all the frenzied activity.

Talbot drove up through the murk in a jeep. The sun was settling down toward the horizon and was throwing the shadows of the men and machinery into bizarre shapes. When Talbot got out of the jeep to check the wire, he was back-lighted by the sun. It appeared as if his shadow were straddling the wire.

Priest rolled onto his belly and put his sights on the specter. His shoulder jerked back as if from the recoil of his weapon. Talbot could not see Priest. No matter, they could not see Talbot targeting each of them in turn.

Crowded in a confined bunker, incoming constant, soldiers talk, Maria. Not of the past, nor the future, not to escape the shelling, but to remember home.

None of the other Marines had writing paper. Perez composed a letter to her, anyway.

I quit college and found work to pay father's medical bills. You, compañera, realized I would be drafted. Both of us knew many families with *sangre* in uniform and there were KIAs. The odds were clear. Chicanos from the university and the barrios protested.

The day for induction came. I went through the routine in dread. I felt like an Indio watching the Spaniards burn sacred books. I saw racks of skulls. The pioneers were drawing the wagons in a circle.

Soldiers talk to forget how they are changed by incoming. How can I ever go back, Maria? I cannot reconcile what I have become. Now I understand why I threw myself into my studies and read for hours.

Before Talbot sent me north into full combat, I went on patrol to a village named Four-Miles on our maps. The medic, Kirsch, found a young girl who was in a coma. Malaria, typhoid, plague—the corpsman couldn't say. Her father wouldn't let Kirsch treat her. He chanted prayers for the dead. The medic wanted to take her to a field hospital. Her father said keep her at home to die with her ancestors for luck.

I put my rifle to the villager's head. By what right did he condemn his daughter? Why should he decide?

"Put down your piece, Bro," my friend Hendrick urged. I can talk with Hendrick. We understand.

The village was Four-Miles on our maps. The war ran by remote control. Heat, flies, full light boiling. Who decides who lives or dies? I tried to remember. Felt buried alive.

"Hey, Fortecca," someone shouted at him as he came out of Talbot's office shielding his eyes from the painful brightness. Fortecca blinked and reached for the folded cap in his back pocket. "The lumber and the empty drums," the man said to Fortecca, "what do you want done with them?"

"Put your address on the shit and mail it home," Fortecca lashed out.

"Well, leave the shit there," the other man told Fortecca.

"Talbot will talk to you later. He'll tell you what to do."

Fortecca pulled his cap down on his head, jerked it right and left until it was centered on his head, and then reshaped the brim into an approved curve. "You. Come here!" Fortecca shouted. The brim shaded his face from the sun and he could see the man walking toward him with measured easiness. "What's that on your lapel?"

The man reached up with his right hand and brushed at his collar. "There's nothing there."

"Just those insignias," Fortecca told him.

These words brought a questioning look. Fortecca moved to close the elenchus. "Just some blacked out metal on your collar that says you're a lance corporal."

"What do you mean 'blacked out?' " The man's face stiffened and he glared at Fortecca, watching his every move.

"Hey," Fortecca said slyly, "you miss the point. You see this?" Fortecca turned down his lapel. "This means I put out shit, and what you've got on your collar means you take it. Of course, if you want to get written up and see the Old Man, I can oblige."

"Yeah, I understand," the other man said slowly, "Corporal."

"We understand each other then. Now, you and the others can move those barrels and lumber away from the noncoms' quarters and stack them beside the nearest shitters over there." Fortecca pointed grandly in the direction of the latrines. "Oh, make sure you don't get too much sun."

For a moment, the man's expression was dangerous but then his face went impassive. "All right, Corporal," he answered, did a negligent about-face and walked away.

Fortecca watched the man walk away, defiant and easy. Just like that fucking Hendrick. Nigger. Fortecca wiped the sweat off his forehead with a cuff and surveyed the camp. A few more tasks and the camp would be secure against attack. The camp was battened down and ready. The sun was slipping away. There was no time now to dig holes for Talbot's additional shitters. The non-coms would have to make do with the smell. Fortecca started walking, laughing at his joke.

As Fortecca cut through the rows of enlisted huts, he saw Priest and two others sitting on the steps of their tent. He turned and walked over to them. "Priest, we've still got watchtowers to sandbag."

"We just came off patrol, Fortecca."

"Yeah, I know, but those towers mean our ass."

"You've got your own men," Priest said. "We did our job and didn't ask for any help from you. We're taking a blow."

"You heard Talbot," Fortecca replied. "No one's finished until we're all finished."

"All right, give us five minutes and we'll be there."

"You refusing an order?" Fortecca flared.

"Fuck off," Priest said, his voice rising. "You just want to push us around."

"I've got more time in grade than you and I'm in charge of a detail. I'm ordering you."

"You're what?" Priest said and rose to his feet.

"I'm ordering you to . . ."

"You're ordering shit, Lifer."

Fortecca took a step toward him. "You want me to make you."

Priest's face got red.

"Don't, Priest," Isaacs said and stood up. "A couple of bags . . . a bad dream."

"Let them go, Isaacs," Lieck taunted from the steps of the hut. "Let's see if Priest is more than words. That's ignominy. I-g-n-o . . ."

"Come on, Priest," Isaacs told him.

"I won't force you," Fortecca told Priest. "I'll let Talbot do that."

Isaacs placed a hand on Priest's shoulder. "Let's go," he

murmured. "Not another court martial."

Priest turned abruptly and began to walk away. "Hey, Prince," Lieck called after him, "how do you like this scope?" Hotshot college boy. Open your mouth. Get yourself thrown in the stockade.

Lieck slapped his cap against his leg and watched the dust fly. Keep beating your gums and I'll watch you burn. The Sarge wants me or I wouldn't be in the leper's hut with you. But I'm playing ball. That counts.

His body ached in the dying sun as he lifted sandbags up to Isaacs. Priest imagined Talbot or Lieck sneering at him and he wanted them dead. Why was he sandbagging watchtowers when the enemy was inside the perimeter?

The war was lost—Priest knew after four months in country, four months into his tour of duty overseas. Fighting guerrillas is not like your WWII pictures, father. The good guys versus the bad. Armies shoot it out and right prevails. In a guerilla war anyone can be the enemy. You have a strategy: they have a cause. To be victorious you have to be willing to kill everyone. Firepower secures territory and ensures mobility. Then you control another culture. So the war is never won. Areas are secure by day. At night you entrench behind barbed wire and shoot anything that moves.

Why couldn't his parents see that this war and the old army photographs weren't the same? They would not kill women and children. What about Talbot? Lieck would do anything to survive. Billboard slogans about America left them blind.

Priest wondered what he could say to his folks. My life is not like the old pictures in your house. I don't want to take them down and put up my own. Taking your place is not the point. I can't. Something happened when you made me go and combat made it plain. I see through my eyes and through yours as well. I am double, both you and myself at the same time, and will never have your sense of home. Many times I felt like an interloper in the house. You loved me. Yet the two of you shared a secret and could not let me in. The secret was in the pictures and part of the walls. Life is single and entire for you in a way that my existence can never be. For you, truth is memory—the exactness of old pictures on a mantle. There is comfort there I understand. I am a chorus a picture can't express.

Talbot is out to kill me. He has a sense of purpose and I call him into question. He'll tell you what he thinks and give you warning the first time you cross him. After that his conscience is clean. Lieck believes in nothing but his prick. He'll tell you anything you want to hear to get his way. Maybe he is right. Who he is so diminishes me that I could kill him for it.

After his father turned Priest out of home, he stopped going to classes. Old gestures did not matter. The future vanished like a trace of early snow. Going underground to escape the draft seemed the only way. But he had been honest with his parents and himself and could not break the law. He could flee the country for sanctuary or refuge. What about Canada or Sweden—become an exile twice from family and from homeland? He was aching from one sentence of banishment. Leaving his country meant abandoning hope.

He got his draft notice. Priest held the unopened letter and could not move. No need to open it. He heard a car door slam, jet noise overhead. The envelope had an oily feel and there was the smell of pictures in pasted albums. He started walking. The letter was in one hand. At times he recognized where he was, then the frame jumped and he was nowhere. He wanted to run, to block out the world, to stop thinking. Jumbled impressions assaulted him. The only constant was the pain. Dying in combat was the final exile.

At times, he noticed people in the streets and he wanted to scream: we're going through the motions and underneath we're dying. Love means compulsion. Responsibility guilt. Freedom is the privilege of always being right.

He came to and was standing near his parents' home. They were a unit in the photos, not individuals. He thought he saw shadows in the den. Maybe his parents were one sort of image and he the reverse. They cancelled him out leaving a baffled and imaginary spook.

"What, Priest?" Isaacs said. Isaacs was looking at him. "You said something?"

Priest could not talk. Isaacs was not holding his own.

"Daydreaming?" Isaacs asked.

"I guess, I guess. Let's fill a few more bags," Priest said. "We're almost done."

Priest used his entrenching tool, while Isaacs held open burlap bags and shook them to settle the earth. After they finished, the two walked to the command bunker where they had left their web belts and canteens. They sat down in the dust, their backs against the sandbagged wall of the bunker. Isaacs spat out a mouthful of chlorinated water. He looked across the compound and wrote in the dust.

"What will people make of this? I mean when people look back at this war. What are they going to say?"

"This will be a forgotten war."

"We could die here, Priest."

Priest could not look at Isaacs. He felt a tightness in his throat and the objects around him seemed to shimmer ominously in the dissipating heat. "I'll keep my head low," he finally answered.

Isaacs let dust fall from his cupped hands. "Nothing has a purpose. When the Light died, God renounced creation. Man is alone and will waste this planet."

Isaacs was slumped over and there was no life in his eyes.

Suddenly, men were shouting behind the bunker. Priest leapt up and ran to the sound.

A group was circled around some bundles of burlap bags.

"What?" asked Priest.

"The bags," someone shouted.

"Bunker four killed a snake two days ago. Now this," Lieck said, moving away from the others.

Priest picked up a piece of two by four near the bunker in the dirt.

"Come on, come on, let's do something before it gets away," Priest urged.

"You're not afraid of a snake, are you?" Lieck taunted.

"Yes," Priest told him.

The men hung back. Someone meowed. "Come on!" Priest urged. "If it's a snake and gets away . . . One of you pull the bags on the left and I will get the stacks on the right."

But no one moved. Priest looked at them. He stepped forward and took hold of bundled stacks of empty bags. Another man moved to the other bundles.

"Now," he shouted. The bags flew back.

"A rat," Lieck said. "Jesus, it's big."

The large gray rat did not move. Its breathing was rapid and irregular. "Too much food," someone joked.

"It's sick," another replied with disgust. "Must be poison Kirsch put out. Let it die."

"It'll only hide somewhere and stink," Lieck said. "Kill it, Priest."

Priest slapped the board against one of his boots to knock off the slippery deposit of caked earth and the film of dust. The rat jerked convulsively at the sound, but did not run. Cautiously, Priest worked around the rat and approached it from the rear. When he was only a few feet away, he raised his bludgeon slowly. Then he snapped the board down.

The rat shrieked and leaped forward at the circle of men. Its back legs were paralyzed and it spun in a slow circle. The soldiers kicked at it hoping to stop the twitching. Finally, the rat shuddered and went still.

The men stepped back, scuffing their boots in the dust. Thin blood oozed from the carcass. Some of the men spat because of the blood.

"Get some kerosene," someone said. "We've got to burn it."

The lull after combat is the day after a binge, Hartman recalled. Empty, tapped out, nothing registers. A grunt's as flat as stale beer. The body is borrowed. Thinking is clear jello. The weight of feelings and a sudden quiet put you half a step behind yourself.

I can turn out O.K., Hartman had reassured himself after the body on the wire came to life and nearly killed him. If I can just get out of combat, I'll be all right. He rinsed out his mouth over and over until the taste of the close call was gone. Got to get away from Point and Dibbs and the bodies in the wire. He had stopped shaking.

Hartman had stripped off his shirt and soaped down after the close call. The cold water flushing the clots and fragments of bone and brain didn't faze him.

He went back to his bunker. The cigar box with the money for Dibbs was on his cot. The box was full of military script from many of the other Marines who saw what Dibbs was doing. Quickly, Hartman put it underneath his cot. There was a blind quiet that helped him forget. But it was his rotation for patrol and Dibbs put him on the point. No one told Dibbs about the cigar box with the money. One of them, either Hartman or Dibbs, would be dead soon, anyway. Stay out of the crossfire. Hartman could see in the dark. He was charmed. They went out several clicks and set an ambush. Nothing. Again they moved out, circled round and still not one shot. Once back in camp, the men whistled and talked about Santa Claus. The enemy was up to something. Too quiet. Hartman couldn't sleep, not because of the enemy, but because something was waiting at the wire. He kept trying to figure what would undo the silent desolation.

Barrages from howitzers started up and sucked the air

from his lungs. The dragonships poured down liquid light to the south. It was closer now. Someone ordered madfire or maybe it just started. All around the perimeter there was outbound—M-14s, M-79s and the hacking of the M-60s. Someone tossed Willy Peter into the brush and the burning phosphorous flung rainbow circles at the night.

I'm all right. I can be O.K., Hartman kept thinking. And Hartman saw Point in the illumination from the madfire. He tasted blood and looked away.

"Goddamn it, Point. Goddamn it. I don't owe you."

Point was gone when he looked up and the battlelight took him in. Point wasn't out there. Point was him.

The muzzle blasts, the upward whoosh of flares, the pop, then the reddish glint. It was all wrong. The wire was in the wrong place. Dibbs was waiting to shoot him in the back. He had to get Dibbs before he broke through.

The Board of Inquiry had nothing to go on but a fragging. The more they found out, the less they wanted to hear. The Board was made up of combat veterans who had all been in tight spots. Combat pinwheel, troops put on the point patrol after patrol: a veteran of three tours shot in the back. Right off the Board knew the unit had to be shut down and mailed away. They remembered the kid who could not keep still when he testified, twisting and turning, a sort of frozen grin on his face, his eyes set back and gleaming. A new adjutant snapped at him about respect for the dead. The Board knew what they were seeing.

"Respect. Yes Sir. Why the legal talk? We share the secret of the uniform. Nothing's real except the killing."

No one had seen anything. No one had anything to say. There was madfire and what was one more explosion from the grenade.

The outfit was disbanded and transferred separately to the rear. Everything was hushed up. If the newspeople found out, more bad press. Command would take heat and the politicians would have a field day. Close the book and leave history off the page.

3

The day burned down in cloudy embers. The sun flared above the mountains and slipped away in angry reds. The trucks drove up to the command bunker to take the men to chow. The troops clambered aboard, metal trays, cups and utensils strung from their belts on strands of stiff wire. The cooling air was strewn with tinny, abrasive noise that died out against twilight's blued gun-metal sky.

"Two days since I've seen you eat," Hendrick said to Isaacs at the messhall. Since the patrol and the near disaster in the rice paddies, Isaacs was too quiet. "There's steak tonight," Hendrick said. The smell of the meat blew over the men in line. Rebo had kept Hendrick talking when he was down.

"I turn my head or close my eyes," Isaacs said, "and when I look again the shapes are gone. Something's in the dark waiting for me."

Hendrick knew others who went over the edge. "It's just the wire," Hendrick told him.

"When I look for them, they're gone," Isaacs continued. "I can't sleep. They will come out of the dark and I won't be ready."

Hendrick remembered a woman who had lived on his street when he was a kid. She wore the same tattered clothes and shawl the whole year. Dressed in black, she rummaged through the streets and garbage cans. She talked to herself of sweet Lord Jesus. Everyone was poor, but no one else picked through the trash. Hendrick heard that she sold the cans and bottles for scrap and gave the money to her church. Children teased the woman and it was bad to see little kids make fun of what they did not understand. He pitied her lost look and blank eyes, but he was angry that someone could be brought so low as to stoop in people's trash.

City officials came and took her away. Harmless old woman, muttering of God and the Second Coming; she was put away somewhere. The brothers on the street told him she died. Maybe that was when he started wanting out.

"I'm here and not here," Isaacs said. "Does that make sense?"

Hendrick began picking at his fingernails so that Isaacs could not see his face. He was worried. What could he do? Isaacs prayed to the God in Rebo's Gospel songs, a God who brought the comfort of His love. Hendrick heard people pray when he was small and once he had prayed too. He didn't want to be on his knees. He wanted to do for himself and get out.

"Nothing is going to march out of the clouds and set life right for us, Isaacs. We've got to hold on."

Hendrick held up two steaks and slapped them down so that they sizzled loudly against the red-hot grill. Before he boarded the bus for bootcamp, Rebo took him out to eat. Afterwards, Rebo bought some fine cognac and they had a few drinks to get loose. The liquor soothed Hendrick's nerves a bit and Rebo walked him to the station. Hendrick had already said goodbye to his parents, no need for them to leave off working.

"You take care, Hendrick. Find people you can trust, no matter what color. Combat puts people on the point alone. Stuck there, you'll never get home."

Hendrick coughed because he couldn't talk.

Rebo put the cognac in Hendrick's carry-on bag.

They shook hands. "Group with the Rainbows, my man: all we have is each other."

Hendrick gripped Isaacs' shoulder. "You've got to eat. You're my friend. Don't fade."

Talbot walked slowly around his room, letting his dinner settle. The steak was good but too well done. He farted and felt his stomach ease. As he sat down on his bunk, he looked at his watch and cursed to himself. Still early. There was plenty of time for beer. He had to go light on the booze. He would check out the outposts later in the night, and he did not want to sleep heavy. He yawned and looked around his room. Absentmindedly, he wound his watch until he felt a sharp pull at his wrist. He saw a hair wrapped around the winding screw. He pulled off the watch and rubbed his skin. Then he smoothed back his arm and replaced the elastic band.

He expected her, as she lay in the coffin, to reach back and smooth her hair. She was always at her hair, brushing it, combing it down over her forehead and hiding her face. She would flip it down over her face, shake it back and begin her long even strokes. If she caught him looking at her, she would hum to herself and her eyes would go dark. She would work hard until her hair was close and glossy against her scalp. He would not have been surprised to see her hand go back, even though she was dead. She was older than he remembered her. But not so much older that her face seemed different than he recalled it, all angles and cheekbones.

When he thought that he had looked at her long enough in the open coffin, he went back to his seat. A few of her friends came up and offered him their cold wrinkled hands and shook his solemnly. He wanted to laugh at them and ask how much longer they gave themselves to live.

The funeral service was short but seemed to drone on without a let up. She was buried quickly. All he remembered was the dull thud of the moist clods striking her coffin. It was a much different sound than the loose scrape of dry clay in this wasteland. When the funeral was over, his brother came up and offered to buy him a drink. That was a stupid thing to do with other people watching and the Old Lady not fifty feet away. But Talbot did not want anyone to think that he was choked up and he did not refuse. His brother wore a suit with sailor legs and his hair curled over his collar. He looked like a thirty-some-odd fairy gone to seed.

Either he was not used to the hard stuff or the quick flight back to the States had thrown his body out of kilter. He had a buzz on after the third drink. He did not feel like leaving the bar right then, and he had to stomach the talk. His brother told him that he was a geologist.

"That's an up and coming profession," Talbot answered, trying to keep the contempt out of his voice. The world was burning and this fool was asking rocks their age. Talbot never insulted a man who bought him drinks. So he held his tongue and sipped his whiskey slowly and tried to clear his head.

While the two of them drank, his brother was looking at him strangely. Talbot caught his brother peering his way whenever he put up his glass. At first, Talbot thought it was the booze affecting his brother. A few drinks threw the mind out of gear. Talbot knew that men act strangely when the wheels spin in their heads.

Finally, his brother looked him full in the face and said, "John, we don't know each other."

Talbot laughed but caught himself. It might look bad if someone knew his mother had just been buried. He was in uniform.

"Forget my first name," he answered. "My name is Talbot."

His brother talked about their family. Talbot did not get the gist of what he was saying. Then right out in the open, his brother said he was not sad that their mother was gone. That pissed Talbot off. What he was saying sounded wrong. Talbot had to put his right hand around his glass. He could not figure out why his brother would talk that way.

When his brother went on to say that he, Talbot, felt the same way about the Old Lady, it was too much. Talbot cut him across the face with the back of his hand. His brother's eyes went hard, but his hands stayed on the table.

Out of nowhere, his brother talked again about the universe running down and freezing up. All that kept a person alive was his relationships with the people he cared for. Their family, the three of them, had failed, and both brothers had never learned to care for anyone but themselves.

Talbot walked out on his brother and checked in at the nearest base. All he could think was, I am a fool for risking my life for people like my brother. Talbot was ready to quit the States and get back to where life was real.

Perez saw Cooper walk into the hut out of the uneasy silence. There was no incoming for now. The naked bulbs glared hotly and the men turned toward him as his shadow tumbled from the walls.

"Communications took a direct hit," Cooper told them. "The blast caved in the bunker. Two dead. Someone's moaning and they're trying to dig him out without burying him. Command is calling retaliatory strikes: B-52's and napalm."

"This fucking war," someone said.

"The KIAs?" another voice inquired.

"The Exec was zapped."

"Dying quick was the best I wished him. He was a manual-mouthing son of a bitch."

"Keoki bought it."

"Keoki wasn't assigned to communications."

"He was making a patch call to Hawaii."

"A week, he told me this morning. A week to home and no one would ever make him leave the Islands again."

"Why him? Snuffed by madfire. Someone shoots blind and someone dies."

"Stupid war in this god-forsaken place."

And silence caved in the hut.

Out of the dim twilight, before he reached his hut, Hendrick heard his name. Someone hissed close by. He stopped and waited. Hendrick finally saw someone sitting on the low square of sandbags that served as protection for anyone who had to clear the hut in a hurry.

"Who goes there?" he asked the shape.

"Come down," the voice said.

Hendrick knew. "What, Priest?" He had to hold the metal cup off his tray to keep the two pieces of metal from banging together as he walked.

"The hut was searched," Priest said in a low voice.

Hendrick took a breath and wedged the toe of one boot between two cross pieces of the boardwalk.

"We got the grenade out in time. No one saw us hide it. The hut has been searched before. This check was routine. Lieck might have doubled back and heard us," Priest said.

"No," Hendrick answered after a pause. "We would be in the brig if Talbot thought there was danger. I want to talk about Isaacs," Hendrick went on. "He's not keeping his head down. He's on the point."

"Talbot is out to get him, and Isaacs doesn't seem to care," Priest answered. "He rambles about God being missing, his wife and that monk who set himself on fire. I think he hears voices."

"Don't talk psychology. He's a friend. If we leave him to Talbot, we'll never feel right."

"What are the options? If Isaacs puts in for a transfer, Talbot will ship him north."

"Couldn't Kirsch send him to a hospital ship with some rare disease? Once on board, he could talk to some shrink. One look at him and they'll keep him."

"Kirsch tried that once before, Hendrick."

"But that was a field hospital and Talbot went and brought him back. He told the doctors either prove Isaacs was sick or Talbot would nail him for malingering."

"I'll talk to Kirsch. How come you'll work behind Talbot's back to help Isaacs and don't say anything when he puts you on every patrol. You're not consistent. You've got different rules for each occasion."

"Relax, Priest. You're coming on like some tight-ass intellectual. When you're ethnic, you talk to different people different ways. You speak to the hearing. Can't say jack to Talbot. I can talk better or worse to you depending on the movie."

"Sounds pretty shifty, Hendrick, like street logic."

"See, Blood. You got the idea. Come down from the clouds, and start thinking with your skin. Let me be who I want, and I'll tell you who I am."

"I'll talk to Kirsch, what else?"

"We wait and watch and let what happens set a plan."

"For Isaacs?"

"For all of us. Take the silver spoon out of your ear."

Hartman dreads twilight and the dark especially in Talbot's camp. Light fades and a grunt loses track of things like they were inked over by some presence that just yawns and thinks, my mistake. Even a hand in front of a face gets lost and the emptiness flattens so that you don't know where space starts and you end. You begin hoping the dark is it because if you do see, you're going to come apart in the battlelights. Sometimes you're strung out with the bursts from the machine guns being cleared, the reddish pulsing of the early flares setting lanes of fire at the perimeter. What you are, where you are, how you came to be there, it's all glare and shadows taking shape, falling back to what you can't make out.

Hartman is north again and the snipers are so thick a grunt moves at a run. The troops start looking at him, not saying anything, just looking careful but insistent.

"They can call in napalm. Set down madfire to thin the bastards."

"Come on, Hartman. They done all that. Firepower ain't where it's at. We're talking balance of terror to make them snipers go underground."

No, Hartman thinks. Not again. I won't do it.

Then some new kid buys it, most of the time in the head. And the guys look at him like it's time now. If he gets pissed, they back off quick. Then it's back to watching Hartman again and the rounds from the snipers ricochet, kick up sound like a busted metronome out of sync but still working.

A patrol goes out before twilight. They stop at intervals and open fire in measured fusillades so that Hartman can put night paint on his skin and tape his clothes to his body so that they will not rustle. Electrical tape secures his sling against the stock of his weapon so the noise won't point him out.

The rest of the patrol doubletimes back inside the perimeter shooting off the hip into the brush, zigging, zagging. Hartman is outside the wire listening to night fall.

On a pre-set schedule, some grunt in the camp uses detonation wire to hold a lit cigarette in the open just a fraction too long. Nothing obvious, just a beat too long. A sniper fires at the target knowing that he has to get away quick from the return volley. And Hartman listening, hears the sharp rustle of the brush and moves toward his target.

Only the enemy knows the game and sometimes sets up booby traps and ambushes of their own. How well a grunt listens and hears with his skin is his ass. Hartman stays frozen in place for hours listening, not thinking, not letting his attention wander. All that matters comes through his ears and his hands.

The sniper fires again, breaks and leaves a trail of sound. While he moves, Hartman moves too, slow and measured, feeling for wires or mines. When the sniper stops, Hartman stops. Sometimes, the sniper is too loud and Hartman knows a trap is set. He freezes and waits, does not move, does not think. Most of the time the enemy ambush stays hidden, sometimes not. Someone pisses or coughs or even yawns. Hartman starts moving in slowly and carefully. When he feels close enough, he takes hold of two of the grenades he pre-pared ahead of time to work quick. Under cover of some noise, he pulls the pins, holding the spoons against one palm so that the grenades will not go off. Then he takes one in each hand, sets himself and waits for madfire. When the shooting starts, he lets the spoons go, waits a beat too long and lobs the grenades at his target.

Hartman hears himself breathing. There is the moaning again from the sappers wounded at the wire and Point telling him, "shoot or listen."

When the helicopter lifted off and started south after the Board of Inquiry for Dibbs, Hartman was thinking, now I'll be OK. I can be all right. He watched the landscape flatten out below and felt that maybe he had beat a death sentence. Two people already wasted. Rubbing his hands against his trousers to wipe away the sweat and dust, he figured, I'm getting away from Dibbs and Point. I'm going south, aren't I? I have to, got to.

That is why Hartman hates night. Is he still north or someplace else? Sometimes he is sure. Then at moments in the dark, he isn't. The night cracks open and he falls in.

Perez could never talk to anyone about his background

before he started college. Maybe he was not ready to think about people like Talbot.

Two dead and one buried alive: Perez knows both the KIAs. Does my past staccato like gunfire because I will die? he wonders.

The sanding machine bucked in his hands as the abrasive disc flung dust from the heavy plastic mold. Fine grit spewed into the gloomy warehouse and suspended particles glinted in narrow shafts of sunlight. The owner of the small factory mixed the plastic daily and poured the thick foul-smelling paste into forms. When the fake marble countertops and washbasin settings were firm but still green, they were stripped from their inserts and dried on plywood backing. His job was to sand down the hardened undersides so that the fixtures sat flush against their mountings. Then he buffed the streaked and mottled imitations. One after another, nine and ten hours a day, fabricated sham for a thirty minute lunch, two ten-minute breaks and the minimum wage.

Three years of college turned to plastic. Perez needed work, any job, in order to pay his father's bills. Education—so what? Just keep the line moving. Two more fixtures are behind.

Is buffing plastic existential? If a hungry rat has freedom, can he choose without cheese?

Hegel, meet Plato: Greek luxury, German precision. *Chale* to both you old boys. Mestizo's mind.

The workers in the factory, all underpaid, broke into two groups: a few Anglo supervisors and a larger group of undocumented workers from Mexico. Right away he heard the sneering epithet "Mexican" from the overmen and knew where he belonged. And the Mexicanos included him and yet did not. They poked fun at his Spanish and called him "Pocho." But when they needed someone to speak to the boss about short checks and lost hours?

"*Te llamas Pérez, sí?* You're Perez, right?"

"*No eres mexicano?* You're not Mexican?"

"*Soy chicano.* I'm Chicano."

"*Déjale en paz, Mano. El trabaja como nosotros y tiene corazón.* Leave him alone. He works like us and has heart."

Neither race nor culture, "blood" nor class, lead to peoplehood without effort. Victims of prejudice do not stand together automatically.

Another plot unfolded. One group of undocumented workers became too insistent about unpaid wages. Immigration staged a surprise raid just before payday.

One young Mexicano asked Perez in Spanish to tell someone in authority. "We need our pay. We have families."

Immigration demanded Perez' green card. "What papers," he replied. "I'm a U.S. citizen born and raised here."

"Yeah," the green man said contemptuously. "You talk good for a wetback. Your papers."

"I have a driver's license and an old college I.D."

"These can be faked."

"My draft card then. Does the U.S. draft Mexicans?"

"Come with me smart guy," the officer ordered.

Only because the owner of the sweatshop needed a pair of arms did La Migra release him. Perez went back to work and could not stop shaking.

———

The few bulbs overhead in the huts were switched on. Letters were written hurriedly. Feelings were drawn out and exhausted. Words were proof of another reality half a world away. Some men brooded over the letters they received. They read them again and again trying to grasp the feelings and doubts hidden in the commonplace. How do soldiers answer those they love and bridge distance?

Some already knew the worst. Former ties no longer

mattered to this war. They tried to ignore those who lived on paper.

The night watch was set when darkness finally closed in. The men remembered the day: any noise or movement would draw fire immediately. The men in the huts got ready for the next morning and hoped they would be lucky. Their weapons were cleaned and oiled. Uniforms were laid out and boots were shined. Routine tasks were exhausted leaving the habitual uneasiness that came with darkness. There was nothing left to do but beat time until taps.

Dearest Sarah,

I am in shadows. I feel abandoned and I cannot pray . . .

Isaacs stared at his letter thinking Sarah was too far away. Why burden her with what I can't write? Maybe if we could talk, I might understand why God, the Light, is a question. Why do I feel as if He has fled and that God's silence is not the issue but my sense of loss?

If Sarah and I could share, she would tease me like she used to. Remember you are frail and God is Above. She learned that from her mother who kept her father down to earth. The ministry means service, not being sure.

People are Cain's offspring. Eaters of flesh. Destruction fills our sense of loss. God has renounced us and has withdrawn. We are broken on a wheel of time until we make earth a desert. Who weeps now that God is fled? What is there to lament? Not humankind. There was some smell he did not want to remember. Maybe himself.

The corded bulbs in the dug-in hut began to tether wildly

and a rolling concussion jarred the hootch as if it were shaken by an earthquake. Cooper and Fernandez stood up and listened. Without a word, Fernandez rushed out of the hut. He came back and pointed upward with quick jerks of his arm.

"The B-52's are hitting the ridges."

The group of men grabbed their gear, went outside and took up positions. Perez had learned to "rev up" while he was in the open and he was puzzled while Fernandez strolled to a trench nearby. Fernandez noticed his uneasiness and told him that the camp would not come under fire while the bombs fell. The two men sat on a lip of gashed earth and watched the airstrike retaliate for the enemy's earlier barrage. The evening pulsed around Perez and sucked at the air in his chest. The bomb bursts came in succession and sometimes followed so closely that Perez could not catch his breath. At first, he was ready to leap into the trench if there was incoming, but then the ridges exploded into enormous palls of fire and dust. No counter fire, and he was transfixed by the devastation.

Perez had seen strikes before and knew the bombers were at too great an altitude to see. The flat quality of the evening light and the dampness of the cooling air threw the bomb hits into hypnotic patterns. The air quivered, firmed into a flash of fire, then congealed into a shock burst which slammed outwards, thinning against the surrounding atmosphere. Then the hills blew apart and boulders, trees and pillars of dust flew up as if a giant bore were ripped from deep within the ground. The whole ridge seemed to lift in slow motion and settle into rubble.

Out of the corner of his eye, Perez saw Fernandez wetting a handkerchief from his canteen while he talked to himself. Without thinking, Perez slid into the trench, readied his rifle and faced his partner.

"*Qué haces, Fernández*? Don't go weird on me."

Fernandez looked at him. "Napalm, Perez. The B-52's

are almost done. You got one of these?" He waved the wet cloth in mock truce. Fernandez slung his rifle over his shoulder and jumped into the foxhole. "You got a rag, Bro, or do you want to be a fire-eater? Unlock your jaw, Man, I'm not tripping."

Perez shook his head.

"Your cap then."

Dumbfounded, Perez took his folded cap from a back pocket and Fernandez wet it from his canteen.

"Nothing gets to me like the napalm. I don't know why. Maybe cause New York fires are an old fear of mine. Coño, Blood, I hate waiting on the flames. Burned alive has got to be the worst ticket out." Fernandez cocked his head and hunkered low in the trench. "They're coming."

Perez was listening for the roar of jets, but when the Phantom burst over the closest ridge, he jumped back against an earthen wall.

Fernandez clamped the wet cloth against his face.

The next jet followed immediately, so low that Perez saw the cylinders tumble from the aircraft. He ducked down, but still saw flames shoot upward beyond the trench and felt a blast of heat. Perez hunched down even lower. Another Phantom flashed overhead close enough to bayonet. Then he saw the pods of jellied gasoline spinning toward him and went prone and pressed against the front wall. The noise of the aircraft roared painfully in his head and he heard no explosion. But suddenly a hot blast choked with thick smoke and the fumes of napalm were all there was to breathe. He felt his uniform but there was no fire and pressed the wet cap against his face. Fernandez was coiled like a fetus and Perez saw his eyes darting above the handkerchief.

He heard again the wail for the dead and lifted his head so that he could hear his name. Perez rose up slowly until he could see over the rim of the trench. The canisters had fallen just beyond the perimeter and everywhere outside sheets of fire. He was transfixed while even the barbed steel burned in glowing strands. The fire made him recall the Indians' destroyed codices, skull racks with whitened skulls and the pioneers who seized a continent. He was mestizo and each one of his cultural backgrounds was a legacy of doom. An Asian war, the Indios' blood sacrifice to feed the sun, the Spaniard's bloody cross . . . History was written in blood. All the past was part of the sheeted fire. He was at point zero.

Kirsch set the tray of instruments back into the steam and closed the sterilizer. He heard a rapping sound at the back of the dispensary. He thought at first it was gunfire far off. He walked to the back room and switched on the bulb that hung from the framing of the roof.

"Come in," he said. "I was in front."

The man entered, shading his eyes, looking around the room. "What I've got to say is personal, Doc. I can't let it get on my record."

"You got nailed again?" Kirsch guessed.

"Yeah. The no good bitch gave me the drip."

"Did you wash off with that soap I gave you?"

"I wasn't looking to get laid, Doc. Our truck broke down in a village and she came up and propositioned me. Her price was low but she smelled clean."

Kirsch went over to a nearby shelf and took down a microscope slide. "Go into the middle room. You know what to do."

While he waited, Kirsch went to the front of the dispensary and pulled the man's file. He had no allergies.

"I swear, Doc, I washed off right away when I got back to camp."

"What about rubbers?" Kirsch asked.

"Nah, Doc. I can't get off. Pussy just doesn't feel right in plastic."

Kirsch put on gloves, took the slide on a piece of sterile gauze and prepared it. "Do you have any sores?"

There was no answer. Then the man responded with relief, "No, Doc."

"I'm going to draw blood."

"Stick me again?" the man said to Kirsch. The man put his head around the plywood partition, as he tucked in his shirt. "I hate getting stuck."

"Watch where you stick yourself," Kirsch said, and gathered the tourniquet, syringe, alcohol swab and a blood tube.

"I'm only human, Doc. She got close and grabbed at me."

"Roll up your sleeve and sit here," Kirsch said.

"Hey, Doc, can't we pass?"

"I have to test for syphilis," Kirsch told him. He wiped down the man's arm and selected a vein. He briskly wiped down the spot he selected and stuck in the needle bevel-up. Blood flowed into the syringe when he drew back, and he snapped the tourniquet off. "Hold this swab in place until the bleeding stops." Kirsch put the specimen into the refrigerator.

Kirsch checked the slide under the microscope. "You were right," he said. "Drop your drawers. You get the consolation prize," Kirsch added. "Three million units."

Before the man left, he held out a small piece of tin foil. "Smoke some of this," he said. "You can put it on a cigarette. It brings everything home."

"Thanks," Kirsch said, "but I don't use it."

"O.K.," the man replied with a shrug. "You medical types have to keep your heads on straight. I've got hams and cases of steak. You're welcome to anything in the warehouse."

"Maybe I'll take you up on that," Kirsch said, "when I

make my next run to the villages."

"The offer stands," the man told him as he turned to go.

"Use the soap. One day you'll come down with something penicillin can't touch. Then you'll be wearing your cock around your neck like a medallion."

"Shit, Doc. A fate worst than Talbot. I'll carry the soap with me. Besides, I'm short," he offered and jigged a few steps. "Thirteen mother-fucking days."

There was more knocking at the back and the man crammed the foil into a pocket and rushed out the front door. Priest came in, looked around and waited.

"It's O.K.," Kirsch told him. "Some grunt with the clap who doesn't want it on his record."

Priest walked to the front door of the dispensary, then came back. "Isaacs is going off the deep end."

"I know. I can't figure what to do. Talbot won't let him out of camp unless he's shot or so sick he's dying."

"He is dying. What about a hospital ship?"

"Our last try was a bust. After all the scamming, there was no psychiatrist at the field hospital. They just wrote down stress neurosis and shot him full of tranquilizers. Talbot got the word and hauled him back. Isaacs was supposed to be in the towers that night. You took his watch. You and Hendrick."

"Isaacs isn't shirking. He stares off into space mumbling about the end of the world."

"How can we get him to a shrink aboard a hospital ship? Isaacs won't fake an illness."

"Something has to be done now."

Kirsch took a bottle off a shelf and took a pull. He grimaced and swallowed water for a chaser. "I would say he has some strange V.D., but Talbot would see through that." He offered Priest the bottle.

Priest shook his head but changed his mind. "Water?" Kirsch gave him the canteen. Priest gagged and coughed but held the medicine down.

"Think some more," Kirsch told him. "I will too. I talked to Talbot today."

"Like being at the wire in the dark," Priest replied.

"You can't stand another watch for Isaacs if he gets bad. Talbot will be checking posts from now on."

"I figured he would find out. He knows everything that happens in this camp sooner or later. I bet it was that fucking Lieck."

"No matter. He's on the rampage because an attack is close. If he finds you trying to cover for Isaacs, he'll ship you, Hendrick and Isaacs north."

"Rat's ass. Why's he trying to kill a mixed up kid."

"You tell me. If I start to understand Talbot, I'm MIA. I'll never go home. What's worse than turning into Talbot?"

"Or Lieck. That fucking low life. Anything to get by. King of the rats. When I think of them, the wire starts moving in. I feel the ticking in my head."

Kirsch stood up and paced. "These walls get close after dark."

Priest could almost see pictures on the walls and he said, "Yeah. Home sweet home. Where am I going back to? Maybe when you treat the kids in the villages next time, you can take Isaacs with you. Working with kids might keep him going."

"I asked already. Talbot said no. Besides, he assigned Hartman to me. Talbot's moving him into your hut."

"One more black sheep to make up for Perez. What do you make of Hartman?"

"He works hard with villagers, although he seems stiff and out of place. I don't want to hear his story. He looks like he never got back. Shit," Kirsch said fidgeting. He took another drink. "I'll never get away from here. I don't know anymore what I'll do if I get back. Seems too far away—unreal. Plans get lost. What about you, Priest?"

"Go back to school maybe. Try to learn how not to be an exile. Put down roots if I can find someplace where I fit. Try not to get lost." Priest reached into a back pocket. "I brought back your book, Kirsch. Every time I start, I lose my way. Gunfire breaks out close by, flares go up or I'm just strung out with the wire."

"I used to read a lot," Kirsch said. "Who can read under flares?"

"There's nothing to salvage. Nothing matters. Just survival mongers like Lieck and the rats."

———————

The night was chilly even without a wind. Still no salvos from the howitzers. Hendrick was relieved to be out of the hut. Lieck was a pimp. And the new man, Hartman? He knows what's up. He'd make it on any street. But Hartman's no Rainbow. Hendrick couldn't look at him and feel trust. Better to leave that one to himself and stay watchful, like on the point.

Priest wasn't in the hut. Hendrick wondered where he was. Had Talbot pushed him too far? Naw. Priest wasn't the kind to kill from hiding. And Hendrick knew he would if Talbot left no choice. Even Priest could do it if Talbot kept after them.

Rebo said he sang Gospel because it let him sleep. Now Hendrick understood. The music had no murder in it. There was grief and suffering and killing weight. But no murder. Sometimes the notes played up the scale and the voices blended to take the breath. Rebo was a soldier once but had got by the killing. Hendrick wondered how?

Rebo never said how he had escaped combat: he let Hendrick talk and mostly listened. A few times there were notes. Don't take a step without it being worth the dying. Rebo's line on the perimeter. Whose dying? Don't do anything if you're not willing to lay in the ground? Or did he mean consider who you hurt?

It wasn't the weather but the new man who made Hendrick freeze. Hartman knows what's up. He's a transfer from the north and trying to get past the killing. Talbot won't let him. But Talbot doesn't know the man and he's a step slower, and not as lean as Hartman. The bogy-man, Old Bones— Hendrick shivered. Jesus, it was cold.

His boots against the boardwalk thudded up his spine. The rifle slung over his shoulder was dead weight. He put his hand on the stock swivel and eased the weapon off the bone. No howitzers. Bad sign. Too much quiet, too much night.

He saw shapes in the dispensary, but had to enter. He knocked, was brought in, and saw Kirsch and Priest. Kirsch was Rainbow, someone he could trust, no matter what color. Maybe Priest was too. Hendrick had to take the chance.

"Hey, Doc. Priest. I should have figured you'd be here." Hendrick looked around and saw no one else. He waved Rebo's Hawaiian hand sign at Kirsch, who understood.

"It's O.K. There's only the three of us."

Priest held up three fingers. "We were talking about Isaacs and what to do." His speech was slurred but his eyes were clear.

"You're juiced, Priest. Give me a chance."

They passed him the canteen and the bottle.

"This man has the second sense," Priest said nodding at Hendrick. "You talk to him no matter how careful and he'll find you out."

"Talk to me, Pictures," Hendrick said to Priest.

"No need. You hear with your skin."

Kirsch looked at them.

"Long watches in those towers and troops know each other, right, Doc? Old pictures of home are ghosts."

"We keep drawing blanks, Hendrick. Talbot will push the button on anything we try to do for Isaacs."

"While you two do your mental dancing, Isaacs fades.

I've got two plans." Hendrick looked around and paused listening. "Rig that grenade to look like suicide, and get Isaacs to a hospital."

"No," Kirsch responded. "Talbot would court martial him."

"For trying suicide?"

"Especially suicide. Talbot is in charge and no one gives up. He'll throw the book at him."

"He's right," Priest agreed.

"All right," Hendrick told them. "Then the next time we're on watch, I toss that grenade, knock him out and mark him just enough to get him clear. Who can tell the difference? No one but you, Kirsch. Shrapnel cuts like a knife."

"That plan will work only if the camp is hit and other towers take casualties. If only your station needs a medic, Talbot will nail us all."

"Will you do it, Kirsch?"

The medic looked at Hendrick and then at Priest. "Are you with us, Priest?"

"You know it."

"We have to wait," Hendrick added. "And when we're hit, our plan goes no matter what. We saw nothing on patrol. Everything is too pat. All the villagers were in the fields not saying anything."

"They're out there," Priest added. "The wire was cut clean. Maybe the job took longer than they planned and daylight stopped them before the last strands were breached. Cutting the wire could be a trick, a feint at this camp while they hit some other post that has odds on us.

Hendrick could not keep still. "Damn," he said, and took a drink without the chaser. "A cut tendon in your hand will heal right, Kirsch."

"Surgeons can repair the wound. The hand might not be right. But you might have to do more."

The sling was cutting into Hendrick's skin. He thought

of Rebo and the scars he carried. But Rebo had beat the war. "I've got to," Hendrick said. "If I don't hurt Isaacs, Talbot will take him out one way or another. That's sure."

"They disarmed two claymores at the wire," Priest said trying to give Hendrick a break, "and carried them off. Some dumb son of a bitch on patrol is going to forget about booby traps and Kirsch will bring back parts."

"Let's not give ourselves away," Kirsch told them. "We'll meet at the enlisted club later and drink with the others. Go back to your hut separately and lay low."

"If we don't do something . . ." Hendrick caught himself and left first.

Any more of that hard stuff and I howl at the dark. Hendrick's lips were numb, and when he breathed deep he felt sweat beaded on his face. Kirsch had the right medicine. No chill from the night air. Good he wasn't in the watchtowers now. He'd talk to shadows.

The boardwalk underfoot looked like railroad tracks in the half moon. He had to help Isaacs get away from Talbot or the man was dead. Hendrick's mind was made up. Yet he did not feel like a well-oiled, finely tuned machine that does its job. Hendrick had a hard choice. There was no way to win. He just wanted to keep Isaacs alive.

The rails ran into the dark. Why couldn't he put one foot in front of the other and get free. Once he left this camp, he would never look back. His tour would be dead time. Clever, clever, he thought. Stand here thinking so you don't have to act.

Having to help Isaacs was like trying to get out of the streets. Hendrick wanted to do something, but nothing was enough. Something in him balked. Was he like the lizard that changed colors to match its background in order to survive? Did he want to escape the ghetto or help Isaacs? He needed some sort of enemy to keep going. Without the streets or Talbot trying to grease Isaacs any way he could, Hendrick got lost. He didn't know who he was without an enemy.

He and Isaacs were behind the same wire. People told you who to be. Be a nigger. Be a soldier. Be a man. The brothers on the street wanted him one way. The Marines another. Everyone wanted a tough guy who asked no questions. If you were yourself, they called you weak. If you were different, if you didn't measure up to their name for you, they labeled you reject.

How many nights had he spent searching barbed wire from the towers, not saying anything because, if you're a man you keep silent when you're scared. He turned into a pair of eyes locked on the perimeter, the way he used to walk the sidewalks after dark. Sometimes like a jolt, he thought, you search everything around you, and there's nothing left. You are a sentinel who considers only attack, blind to yourself. His life was outside in the dark, coiled and twisted with the wire.

Putting an enemy soldier in the sights of a weapon was one thing. But someone who was your ally, despite his color: Isaacs was Gospel. Priest and Kirsch must feel as Hendrick did now. They were marking time in shadows, dreading when the shooting would start.

Hartman was in a new hut with different strangers stretched out on a cot and a smell he didn't recognize. The A framing of the roof could only hold him for so long and then his eyes closed and he was off.

Some young kid, there had been too many up north to

remember names, went to battle loaded down with ammunition, grenades, a bayonet so sharp it sliced paper, flares and more. Maybe he figured he could bluff death if he looked fierce. Maybe suddenly he saw the enemy everywhere and wanted to kill them all. Could be the kid liked war movies and T.V. and confused combat with theatre. Lots of shooting, no one gets wasted. Dying is messy with no reruns. Making death imaginary got him killed.

Hartman warned the kid about being on the point. The kid was insistent and declared he could handle it. Trip wires at every level, Hartman warned: on the ground, knee high, right at the chest. Watch for mines and booby traps in the brush. Walk light and feel every step. If the ground is loose, if you catch something out of the corner of an eye, stop, get low and move easy and careful. Don't think. Get outside yourself and let every sense work for you. Hartman caught himself slipping and opened his eyes. Knots all through the two by fours and there were streaks of pitch. Maybe he was smelling the wood.

The enlisted club was open now. Time for a beer. Hartman walked out of the hut of strangers.

When Kirsch tried to turn off the bulb in the back room of the dispensary, the switch broke. The humidity corroded metal. Everything goes bust by remote control. Kirsch pulled his sleeve down over his right hand and held the light bulb steady while he unscrewed it. The room went blood red and then dark. While he waited blind, the night crowded into hearing. A mosquito whined close to his ear—insects were outside. Nothing from the howitzers, no rattle from machine guns. It was early. Voices came out of the dark, rising and falling. Occasionally, he could make out words, but mostly unintelligible snatches of conversation.

Very often, when Kirsch spoke to others or listened to them, the voices left an echo: hollow, distorted unreal. He was trying to peel shadows from blackened, shifting walls.

Poor Isaacs. Or was Isaacs blessed? He couldn't fight, couldn't kill. Some sense of being human came before surviving.

Months ago, two men had quarreled. No one knew for what. One man pointed his rifle at his watchmate. "You haven't got the balls," the man under the gun taunted. They were in formation and the troops around thought they were pulling some kind of trick.

When Kirsch got to the shooting, the victim was lying on his back, his shirt-front soaked with bright red blood. He was shot through the heart and he had no pulse, no respiration. The wound in the center of his chest was clean. Kirsch put the heel of his hand over the wound, breathed into the man's mouth and tried to resuscitate him. Kirsch's response was automatic, he was in a state of shock.

After a few moments, Kirsch saw a dark stain soaking up under the man's shoulders and back. Hendrick helped turn him over and they saw the hole the size of a fist. Kirsch had been forcing fluid out of the wound and the dust underneath the body was a bloody mire. Only after the medical report had described the fatal wound did he stop believing he had killed someone because he had not kept his head.

Kirsch could not talk about the war after the shooting. Night sowed the earth with dragon's teeth and unseen men rose up to attack and send rockets curving in upon the camp. When the rockets did not fall, there was nothing left to do but wait.

When Kirsch dressed minor injuries, he remembered the shooting and the clotted dust. He was efficient and watched the details. A technician of flesh, Kirsch thought to himself. Detach yourself from the others and keep your head in an emergency.

Alone, Kirsch thought, I have always separated myself from others. My job is not the point. It's who I am. I don't want to be close to anyone. I don't want to be disturbed by feelings which depend upon something as frail as life.

Kirsch took a deep breath. How did he come to grips with Isaacs? Death was not mental ambulance chasing now. Talbot would ice someone else he knew, just like Perez. Before the war, Kirsch turned combat and death into a myth to fill a void. Isaacs was in peril, but this time Kirsch could save a life.

"Little Joe, Little Joe," Lieck chanted to himself in a corner of the hut. "My point is four."

Priest was in his cot using a book for cover. He pretended to read, but he was only listening to Lieck and his own thoughts. Long days, interminable nights, tedious routine, constant fear. Isaacs, Lieck and myself: we are together in a hut, but we're cut off from each other. We rasp like bits of broken glass—jagged slivers of empty hopes, prejudice, the assurance of superiority. Lieck rolled the dice, and they clattered against the plywood floor. "Two trays," Lieck went on. "I don't need a six. Come on four."

The men in this hut share boredom and the dust—not our thoughts of war, Priest realized. Disclose nothing. Anonymity means privacy. Do not talk, because bad feelings risk violence. Lieck tossed the dice and they rebounded against a book he had set up for his game. "A niner. Roll again. Speak dice," he cajoled, "any total of four." Priest was a prisoner watching his moods thrown up on a screen. He was trapped on a blank page with no exit. The dice ricocheted crookedly.

"Seven! Crapped out." Lieck surveyed the hut. "Anyone

want to shoot a game?"

No one answered. "Hey," Lieck shouted. "I've got a few bucks of funny money left before next pay-day." He held out a small wad of military script. "I feel lucky. Put up your money for a worthy cause. You! Isaacs, why not try your hand?"

Isaacs was face down on his cot and did not respond.

"Shit, Isaacs," Lieck said, "you must have money?"

Isaacs said nothing.

"You, Priest. Come away from that book. Reading will only make you talk. You already do too much!"

"Cram it, Lieck," Priest shot back at him, and turned a page.

"Why read? Why knot up your mind? Let the dice think for you." Lieck shook the dice in his cupped palms.

"I prefer fuck-books like this," Lieck said, and reached over and held up the paperback he had been using for the dice. "Person X meets Person Y. He penetrates, she lubricates. Everyone comes to a fine conclusion."

Priest placed his open book on his chest and closed his eyes.

Lieck saw his opening. "You like the book?"

"No, not really," Priest answered.

"Then why read it?" Lieck countered.

"Because I want to understand," Priest answered.

"Hah!" Lieck snorted. "What is there to understand. They have a space between their legs we crave. We try to bed them, they trick us into marriage. Men get caught, women feel trapped. All the sexes have in common is a few good fucks before we find each other out.

"Love is grand," Lieck mocked. "Fuck-books are the point. I'd give a week's pay to make my point, but I'm trapped inside this wire."

"Grease up a rifle barrel," replied Priest. "When you're finished, put it to your head."

"Ah, cunt," Lieck went on without notice. "There is a

dispensation between a woman's thighs. Do you put women on a pedestal, Priest, and talk to them about ideals?"

"I never met a woman I could talk to without sex getting in the way," said Priest.

"You don't have to talk at all," tossed off Lieck with a laugh. "Just use your hands a lot." Lieck turned away from Priest and addressed Hendrick, who had entered the hut. "Dice, Oddsplayer?"

Isaacs, Talbot. The two were jangling Hendrick's head. Isaacs was on Talbot's list and wouldn't do anything for an out. Hendrick had an aunt who used to say I am poor but rich in Gawd's love, like a preacher.

"It's time for dice," answered Lieck. He was too keyed up to pay close notice to Hendrick.

"You know, Hendrick," commented Lieck, "I don't think Priest has ever been laid."

"Let me see the dice, Lieck," Hendrick interrupted. Lieck tossed the dice to him. Hendrick ran his fingers over the ivory and shook the cubes in his hands. "Blowing on dice," he said. "Brings me back years. My father would come in late in the evening from his job and there was nowhere to go. He would break out a can of pennies and bank us all for fun. We would roll until the streets went quiet."

Hendrick had learned to always take care of himself. No one made it in Chicago unless he took care of Number One. Priest said, street thinking made you blind. How does a Golden Boy find that out?

Hendrick considered himself poor, not just because his parents never had money, no matter how hard they worked, but because he felt powerless. Things happened and he got sucked along. Priest was upper class and would never feel like that.

Before a man could get free of the streets, he had to escape pursuit. People with money know how to walk slow, because no one is chasing them. Poor people only know how to make rent, how to stretch out the food.

"When I was a kid," Hendrick said, "I walked around in a state of baffled desire. I wanted to be out of a place where the walls always said more money, more food. I wanted the neighbors to stop screaming. I wanted to stop feeling poor. I wanted so many things without knowing that I wanted my whole life to be different.

"When I hit fourteen," Lieck broke in, "I knew I wanted sex. My first fuck . . . Oh, mama. Sex was all desire."

"Only people with money can be discontent," Hendrick went on. "Poor people are unhappy. You got to eat good to have the time for questions."

Talbot acted like a rich man in a poor man's army. He believed in the Corps and didn't care about pay. Hendrick remembered Talbot in his bleak office telling him he was a good soldier. The worst was that Talbot said they were two of the same kind. Isaacs and Talbot. You couldn't get one without the other.

Hendrick rattled the dice loudly in his hands. "I feel like a kid hunched against a wall throwing dice, hearing the streets come out of the dark." Hendrick rolled the dice. One of them hung up crookedly against the wall. "Cocked dice," he said. "I roll again. Craps is blind chance. Nothing controls the dice."

Lieck whistled as if he were amazed and puffed out his cheeks.

Hendrick sat on his cot. Priest went back to his book.

"Dice?" asked Lieck. Hendrick tossed them back. "No takers?" His arm fell. "Condemn me to drink with the masses?" He turned to Priest. "Dull jokes and country music. Deliver us from modal man."

"You make me tired," Priest answered.

"Which only proves that I exist," Lieck replied and left for the enlisted club.

After a while, Hendrick got his rifle and put extra magazines in his back pockets. Priest did the same. The two men slung their weapons over their shoulders and left for the club.

Talbot unfolded his hands from under his head, sickled his legs to his chest, and kicked himself into a sitting position on the edge of his bed. His gut was hard still and when he pinched his waist, there were only a few loose folds of flesh. He hated to think about getting old like his mother. Old skin was leathery and ridged like turkey wattles.

He thought of the turkey his mother had him raise year after year. If the poult was young when his mother brought it home, the bird thought it was a chicken and scratched with the hens. He would laugh scornfully when he saw a big bird with a scrawny neck hunkering down, pecking at the ocher clay.

His mother never let him forget the bird was for killing. If he spent too much time around it, she would wait until he came near and pinch him hard so that her nails dug crescent wounds into his skin. "Things you raise are to eat," she would hiss at him, her lips pinched and mean. If he cried, she got madder, so he learned to shut his eyes and press his lids together with all his might to forget the pain.

She tricked the bird month by month into eating through a section of the fence. When it was killing time, she grabbed its neck and forced the head into an old sock. Once, a butchered bird escaped from the burlap bag his mother had trussed it in. It ran wild in the yard. Talbot thought it would get away and he dived at it and clutched his arms around the beating wings. His mother laughed while he tumbled with the headless fowl, and he listened to her with his face against the bird's breast, feeling the shudders weaken until the body went slack. When he let go and stood up, he saw that he was smeared with blood. He saw his mother approach him, and he covered his head with his arms and hands. There were no blows, only more of her laughter. She stooped and stuck a feather into his hair. She told him he was her Indian.

Maybe tonight would be a good night for cards. He had not done well for weeks and tonight might be his time to shine. He went to his closet and took out a freshly laundered uniform. The shirt smelled like swamp water. He cursed the slant-eyed bitch who did his clothes. She would stand there nodding at him, pretending that she understood what he was saying. Then his clothes came back smelling like shit.

She wasn't good for anything. He offered her fifteen American dollars for a poke. She turned him down. When he spoke to her, she turned toward him and seemed to listen. But her eyes were like smoked glass with no light behind them. He hated it when he caught her eyes on him. Sometimes he would turn around quickly and catch her staring at him when she was supposed to be cleaning his room. She would smile but her eyes would stay dark and watchful. He wanted to grab her by the hair and pull back her head and see fear in her eyes. He did not feel he had the upper hand and he hated her for making him uneasy.

Months ago, a patrol captured a woman without identification. She clearly despised Americans. She was haughty and refused to cooperate, even after a week of confinement. He had her brought to his office regularly for questioning. She said nothing and never looked at him. Once, he put his hand around her face and tried to turn her head toward him. She spat on his shirt.

Talbot cleared the room of everyone, even the interpreter, and posted a guard at the door with strict orders to keep everyone outside. He took out a sharpened bayonet he kept in his desk. He held it to her throat. Her face remained impassive. He drew the blade lightly against her skin, and when she gasped and put her hand to the cut, he backhanded her with his closed fist.

When she regained consciousness, he repeated what he had done. The next time he put the bayonet to her throat, she almost collapsed. He pulled off her black silk trousers and unbuttoned himself. She was still dazed from the blows and she looked toward the locked door. He put one hand around her throat and forced her back on the desk top. She shook her head and tried to move away from him. He hit her. She kept shaking her head when he pressed himself against her. He spit into his hand when she stayed dry. She was a gook and a woman. She should have known her place.

Outside the dispensary in the night, Kirsch imagined himself in the hut, then in a room within the hut; he added the camp and built on. He started backwards and obliterated what was set. All that remained was a medic standing in the dark. Kids' games don't undo war.

Death was the tip of a whip that snapped out in one direction and cracked back—whiplash of consciousness. Being alive was balancing chaos against what made sense right now. Even after making a hard decision, chaos comes again. There was no quiet for the self. What was it Priest said about the war? Banality of evil. Just like death.

No light filtered from the phosphorous into the dug-in emplacement. By battlelamp, Fernandez showed Perez where he had placed the boxes of ammunition, grenades and flares between them. Then he cut off the switch and told Perez to hand him what he asked for. When Fernandez was satisfied with his partner's performance, he picked up the field phone and checked in.

"We clear our weapons in five minutes," he told Perez. "1940 by the dial."

Perez sighted on the darkened bushes beyond the wire, then checked the time. His M-14 was keyed on automatic and the tracer rounds would find the range.

"They'll be out tonight," Fernandez said. "They can't let us think the bombs and napalm will keep them off. They're dug into the hills and now that the sun is gone, they'll come looking for us. They know where we are and we're shooting blind."

The last minutes ran down slowly. "Ten seconds," Fernandez announced finally.

Perez pulled the rifle into his shoulder, braced his legs and Fernandez said, "madfire." He squeezed and the rifle bucked tracers to the mark. He squeezed and backed off until the magazine was expended. And then he changed magazines rapidly, chambered a round and waited. Fernandez was still firing and the ejected shells made a tinny echo against the hard-packed earth.

Isaacs wanted to sleep. Priest and Hendrick left the light on. He tried to close his eyes but the brightness was pressure. He sat up, braced his weight with his hands and stood. He went to the light switch. The bulb flashed dark and, after images, merged into black. He did not wait for his eyes to adjust, but stumbled between the lines of cots, banging his legs.

Hunched over, he moved from one cot to another by feel. He ran his fingers over a footlocker at his feet. The nicks and deep gouges in the surface were his. He lay down, not even taking the time to unlace his boots.

Death comes with no warning, curving in. If he was asleep . . . He closed his eyes. He had not heard the firing begin. Asleep there would be no warning, awake maybe a split-second. Too short a time for anything except the knowing.

A stranger, an outsider and there was no light. He tried to remember Sarah. Dearest wife. Darkness locked him in. She, breaking open around him; he secure. He felt the swelling and relived what had passed between them.

There should be calm, but nothing could save him. He pulled away the blanket, peeling back the foul wetness. The remembrance was a sham. His body was meat.

He was thirsty and wanted to be away from the cot. He got his canteen, drank the few mouthfuls of fluid and wondered if the water was on. If he got up to see, the effort, like everything else, might come to nothing.

Sandy grit was all through the hut. If the hut was swept out three times during the day, the wind blew back the abrasive powder or it was tracked in. Near the steps, the earth reeked of urine. Isaacs saw flares to the north, and as he walked, he noticed light in different sectors. A howitzer fired and the vibration echoed through the huts. He kept to the boardwalk. The water was off. He heard trapped water trickle from the pipe. He put down his canteen and unbuttoned his trousers. He washed himself roughly. When he had finished, he put the canteen to the pipe. The fluid was flat and tasteless. There was no difference between thirst and drinking—all was useless and without meaning.

Back in his cot, he heard gunfire and thought, so what? A flare burst into light outside and reddish glare seeped in. A hand clenched the folds of his blanket, obscene—scaly, swollen like a claw.

The Oddsplayer spread himself across the darkness of the hut, cupped his hands and blew briskly on the dice. "If you lose, you lose nothing; but if you win, you have salvation."

The wager sickened Isaacs. God had fled the world and left him to the Oddsplayer.

The Oddsplayer made faith a melodramatic wager. War and uncertainty were house odds, banked to the Oddsplayer. With a gambler's grasp of fear, the Player wagered for belief.

A machine gun fired close by.

The Oddsplayer compressed against the sound and vanished. "You're not God," Isaacs said. He recalled a gawky self-conscious kid who wanted to be a missionary and save Indians in Peru. He accused himself. You felt abandoned back then and substituted religion for loneliness. You used God to fill your emptiness—that's not faith, that's blasphemy.

A howitzer fired in the distance, and, as if in answer, a flare shot up from the far edge of the camp. Hartman was drawn out by the remnant of moon. The wooden walkway appeared like bleached bones and missing crosspieces gaped like broken teeth. Another flare went up close. The surrounding area was scarred and pitted by shifting zones of light and darkness.

No words carried across the dark. Grunts could talk but never express the feeling of being on the point. Hartman was walking to the wire in the morning's dead light, the rusty wirecutters in his belt. Once the detail gave him cover, he kept his attention on the wire, only the wire. When his hands brushed the body, they snapped back. He cut the body free of the metal strands and used his bayonet to pry the wire from the flesh. He had to take hold of the corpse and pull it into the body bag. He avoided the dead man's face. Even if he had known the man, he would have fired at anyone coming through the wire. He was Hartman's age. Hartman shot him as his foe would have done to him. That was the reason. The wire had been laid down; he was behind. At the point, there's no regret.

Talbot fanned out the cards in his hand. Two aces, spades and hearts jumped out at him. He kept his face quiet so that he would not give himself away. Keeping the aces and drawing three new cards would be his game.

"Jacks or better to open the game, Top. Are you in?" the young sergeant inquired.

"I'll start the game easy," Talbot said. "I'll go a dollar." Talbot was pleased when he was raised two bucks. The pot would be fat and ready for the killing.

Talbot discarded and took up his three new cards. Everyone else took at least two cards. No one had a wired hand. Another ace and a pair besides would set him up. Of course, two more aces was even better. It was his turn to win. He was down thirty bucks.

Life was a card game, always putting him behind. This time the cards were in his favor. Talbot shuffled his cards together face down, folding them one over the other at random. He snapped them up in front of him. The ace of spades was an old card. He saw next what the doctor ordered, the ace of diamonds. Three of a kind was a sure winner. The hands before this one had all been low. The ace of clubs would put away the game. The ten of hearts was a Spic in the woodpile. He lingered over the next card, wishing it right. The three of spades was useless. Three aces was his hand.

Talbot kicked up the bet three dollars. Two players folded. The only man left kicked the bet three more. The size of the bet bothered Talbot. His opponent must be trying to bluff. Talbot knew he was the better man. No one had ever gone to bat for him. He could have been an officer if he had

had the chance. In Korea, he almost had a battlefield commission. His unit held for nineteen hours. The Chinese assaulted their position in human waves, not caring about their casualties. His unit lowered their howitzers to fire point-blank into the massed enemy. The barrels of the machine guns were so hot that the gunners had to cool them in the snow.

The Chinese were on one side, his unit was on the other. Everyone knew their place. No one complained. If a wounded man could fire a rifle, he went back on the line. One man put a rifle to his shoulder when half his face was torn away.

Hartman might think that, just because a sergeant-major sat behind a desk, that he was only spit-and-polish and a pencil-pusher. But Talbot knew what he had been through in Korea was more than anything Hartman could have possibly seen up north. In this theatre, the yellow bastards did not stand and fight. They stole away at first light and made war in the dark.

"I'll see your three and kick it three more," Talbot said to his adversary.

"What have you got, Top?" the young staff-sergeant asked.

"You'll have to waste your money to find out," Talbot told the young jerk. What was happening to the Corps? Punks with faces like a baby's ass, that liked loud music and that had to question everything were his replacements. How could they stand up under fire? A man had to be raised hungry to be willing to fight. A Marine goes for the balls or throat and kicks at the head when his man is down. What did the future matter to him? Everything was falling apart: the country, the people, and especially the pukes who would take his place. The world was wobbling on its axis like a top running down. When the earth stopped spinning, everything would collapse into rubbish. Anyone left alive would have to claw at the earth with bare hands to stay alive. Time would be set right.

"I call you," the staff said. "I won't gut shoot you.

What's in your hand?"

"You won't do shit, soldier," Talbot told him and threw
down his cards. "I've got three bulls."

The kid looked him full in the face. "Not good enough,
Top. I've got a flush."

You fucking kid, Talbot thought, and gripped the edge of
the table hard. He brought his teeth together and clenched his
jaws. When he stood up to leave, he held his head steady on
his neck. "Another time," he said, although the words caught
in his throat. Deliberately, and without haste, he walked out
of the Non-Commissioned Officers' Club. He fought himself
to a standstill, did not turn back and kick down the door when
he heard laughter behind him.

As Priest and Hendrick drew close to the enlisted club,
electrified music and voices took them in. Priest kicked the
toes of his boots against the walkway before entering. Hendrick squared his shoulders and got ready to deal with the
labels the grunts used to keep him invisible.

The Club was supposed to be an escape. The only illumination was from uncovered red bulbs intended to help the
troops relax. They were the same hue as the battlelamps. The
beer was cheap and there was usually more than the ration.

Grunts shuffled in closed circle from table to bar as
many times as the alcohol lasted. Shadowy uniforms slouched
on metal chairs, disembodied hands worshipped cans of beer.
Stretched above, white nylon parachuting undulated in the
breeze that blew through the screened angle of the roof. In the
red glow, the fabric flickered like flames. The shapes below
were consumed in smokeless fire.

Hendrick's skin looked surreal to him in the reddish
glare. White faces everywhere. He wished Perez was back.
Kirsch was coming and Priest was O.K. Still not enough

color to put him at ease. Hartman was sitting alone in a far corner. Troops knew better than to approach. The small table in front of him was already lined with cans.

Priest and Kirsch and Hartman all fought their own wars now. Hendrick's skin put him at the wire long ago. Had he been at the perimeter all his life because of the rage in him? Here he was doing battle for a country which set him apart. Don't blame yourself Hendrick thought. You're trying to get off the bottom. That's the reason you're here. It sounds mercenary. Hendrick laid out his odds. Maybe I'm selling my soul. I'm not defending shit. I'm doing time to do better than my folks. If I don't make it, they're getting my insurance and moving up for me.

People at the bottom need an enemy—that's what enraged Hendrick. Perez understood. He had told Hendrick, you can't blame yourself because you're trying to get ahead and just keeping up. You've got to turn the bitterness and defeat at someone. Why blame yourself when you've got no control?

When Hendrick had to walk through the city after nightfall, every sense was alive. He searched the shadows in his path for something laying in wait. Some person behind him at night was a reprieve. He made quick moves to see if he was followed and checked ways to escape. If he was being shadowed, fear turned to rage. Being on the bottom was enough. He made a plan and confronted the threat. An adversary was familiar territory.

Hendrick and Priest checked in their weapons and went to the bar. The quiet dude behind the counter brought cold beers. Hendrick held out military script as payment. Buying another man's time when he could do for himself bothered Hendrick. He remembered hamburger grease and the smells of short order cooking all over him.

Two successive explosions shook the club, but no one missed a beat, except Hartman who jumped up and was on his way to the door. No one looked his way and no one laughed, except for some grunt. Hartman went over and talked to him. The grunt said Hartman was polite and had asked him not to laugh, only Hartman was jerking slightly and his eyes rolled back in their sockets. There were no more explosions. Their own howitzer rounds must have short-fused and exploded close by.

Someone called their names and the second time Hendrick knew. But they had to keep cool and the bar was neutral territory where everyone drank together. Hendrick threaded through tables and Priest followed. Lieck was with Kirsch and two others he had not seen before. Someone pushed an empty seat at Hendrick and Priest retrieved another chair.

"That's Hendrick," he heard Lieck say over the noise. Lieck pointed at Priest. He lost the names of the two strangers.

Hendrick nodded around the table appreciating the uproar. No need to listen to the others fumble with his skin. His beer was harsh and he felt the cold wash to his gut. He did not want to talk and instead he drew a finger through the moisture on the outside of the can. The displaced film ran down the metal.

"I've got the scoop on Hartman," Lieck told them, keeping his voice just loud enough for them to hear. "I knew he was strange. These two are on R&R from up north and they heard stories about Hartman's former unit." Lieck pulled the pin on an imaginary grenade and rolled it under Priest's chair.

"What a life you rear-guard wonders live," the unknown to Hendrick's left broke in. He was young with sharp features and he drew his lips together as if he were hiding his teeth. His companion looked around the table and smiled to himself.

"Three hot squares a day and cold beer," the first man said. He held up his beer.

"You should see the Officer's Club," Lieck chimed in.

"Fuck those prima donnas," said the first stranger. "Officers corner the best of everything—food, booze, women—and leave us enlisted troops the leftovers. They kill our ass, then go home and tell war stories.

"Officers and enlisted don't figure the same way," Lieck told everyone. "We grunts carry the load of the fighting."

"What shit, Lieck. What risks do support troops face? You should be up north with us." The first man's face looked lean and starved.

Lieck looked down at the table and began to tear off the grimed ends of his nails.

"We're fighting a real war up North. Just before the two of us came down for these three days of R&R, we were hit."

Machine gun fire crackled close by and Lieck got up and walked to the bar.

The first man paused to take a drink. "They scored a direct hit on one bunker. Four KIAs, five wounded. One of my friends was zapped. I'll get a couple of gooks for him."

It struck Priest that the first man was at the movies. The scene called for killing and this macho was ready to square a debt.

Lieck returned to the table in time to hear the last of the performance. Out of the corner of his eye, Priest saw Hendrick fidgeting with his beer.

"I'd like to get some gooks," Lieck cut in. "But, hell, Jensen, I want to make this war in one piece. All your medals won't buy a cup of coffee back in the world."

Jensen's buddy gave Lieck a fishy look, but Lieck was unperturbed.

"Let the enemy do the dying," Lieck countered. "Let's see that 47 again," he said to Jensen trying to change the subject.

Jensen reached under the table and brought out a stubby, menacing weapon. "It's a sweet little machine, Lieck. I'd carry it rather than an M-14 any day. Your friends here," he waved at Hendrick and Priest, "haven't seen my picture." His eyes glinted in the reddish light.

"Show it to them," Lieck tossed off.

The young starved face made a great show of taking a picture out of his shirt pocket and handing it around. Priest passed it on after a glance. Hendrick saw Priest wipe his hands. Hendrick was tired of family scenes: women smiling for the camera and holding babies. Hendrick took it. He saw a man sprawled in barbed wire. A large dark splotch was all around him. The face was swollen and blanched, as if he had drowned instead of being shot.

"My first gook," Jensen announced.

Hendrick felt the square of paper in his hand.

"The sappers tried to storm the wire, but we stopped them. I got him with my first burst, but he still kept coming. My second burst put him down. He ripened on the wire until morning. I took no chances on booby-traps. I shot him with my polaroid."

Hendrick handed back the picture and put his fingers to the wetness of the beer can.

"He kept coming though." Jensen put up his hands, as if he were reconstructing the attack. "He must have been on something. Two full bursts . . ."

"I'm going back to the hut," said Priest, and got to his feet. His voice was sharp.

Jensen looked at Priest, but Priest turned and moved off.

Hendrick took a long swallow ignoring the bite. The beer was not strong enough. He drank the rest. "I need another beer," he told the table.

"I'll fly, if someone buys," Lieck said.

"I need to piss," Kirsch commented. "I'll go."

Hendrick looked over at the corpsman rocking the can on the table. Kirsch got up.

"Jensen, Willard, you need another beer?" asked Lieck.

"I think we'll go back to transient quarters," answered

Jensen.

"Have another beer," Lieck prodded.

"No, got to get a full night in the sack." Jensen rose from his chair, threw back his head and guzzled his beer. Willard got up with Jensen. He looked over the others and waited for Jensen to take his leave.

"Take her easy," Jensen said and the two men left the club. Lieck went to the bar and ordered six beers.

"These all for you?" the barkeep asked.

"I'm with the heroes from up north," Lieck told him.

"I thought I saw them leave," replied the barkeep.

"They got choked up with the fellowship and decided to go piss on some flowers. How about six of your coldest?" Lieck went back to the table.

"Your friends?" Hendrick asked Lieck when he got back to the table.

"I know the corpsman in their unit," Kirsch explained. "They looked me up."

"Could you do a watch with Jensen?" Hendrick asked the medic.

"Anything except my reflection."

"Priest is a silly bastard," interrupted Lieck. Lieck crushed his empty can, pressing against the surface with his thumbs until the metal can bent in the middle. He used his palms as a vice and flattened the ends together. Lieck placed the crushed can on the table and gave it a flick of his fingers so that it wobbled back and forth. "Let those fools believe they are the apocalypse. As long as they are up north, not me, they can tell all the war stories they want."

"What time is it?" Hendrick asked.

Kirsch searched through his shirt pockets. "2150."

"That's very good," Lieck said. "Now what time is it?"

"Nine-fifty."

Lieck stood up. "Bong . . . bong," he clanged.

"Lay your heads down and sleep

howitzers won't make a peep
soldiers must get their sleep
unless they get had."

Hartman sat back down at his table, cursing himself for forgetting where he was. You're not in combat. No one better laugh. Better to be paranoid than dead.

One kid who wanted on the point was all bandoleers of ammo, grenades clipped to his utility belt and flares, a gleaming bayonet sheathed in a homemade scabbard bought in Okinawa. Hartman called him Short Round, which the kid didn't like. Hartman hoped the nickname would make the kid forget the movies. That handle might piss him off enough to make him careful. He was smart, just stuck in matinees.

It was a burst from an AK-47, Hartman recalled. Not a sniper, not a boobytrap. Some regular on the other side let the point man get right up to him before he fired, which means he was trying to be dead too.

The kid exploded. A grenade blew and touched off flares he carried. A ragged piece of trunk was lit up from the burning flares and blood and bits of meat spewed everywhere. Hartman nailed the enemy from his muzzle blast. The grunt behind him was going, "Jesus, God," over and over and the flares would not go out. What was left of Short Round kept burning—mixed with phosphorous and the stench of flesh.

Hartman had to take charge because the light meant incoming and no one was doing anything. He threw off the flares still burning, grabbed the legs of the corpse and dragged the kid away from the illumination. He tried to carry him, but there was no other way but to drag what was left in the dark. The scraping sound rasped to the bone.

"Hey, Pussy," Dibbs called the grunt who could not shake off what he had seen. "You owe your friend. Get hold of yourself and do your job."

After Dibbs had left, Hartman told the kid, "Be smart. Think for yourself." The grunt did not understand. Dibbs kept pushing him to even the score. Another casualty a week later.

Perez heard Fernandez reaching into the box of ammunition. Each cartridge made a dull snap as Fernandez reloaded the magazines.

"Jail would have been smarter," Fernandez said. "I would have done eight months probably. The dude I cut wasn't hurt bad. Him and his boys came on my turf and called me out. The judge didn't care. All he saw was my rapsheet and hard time. But shit, I was a loser. I would have cut you, Hermano, or any other Blood on a bet. I seen enough people now to know that some of us are twisted inside. That sergeant who set you up and shipped you here is a warped motherfucker. It don't matter why, he just is."

Perez had wanted to kill Talbot but could not.

"War is like the street," Fernandez went on. "There's you and them, the ones outside the wire. You team with people because without hands you're dead. And then you start acting out a loyalty game that's only as strong as the enemy."

"Make me nervous, *compadre*."

"*Vaya, pana*, I'm as solid as stone as long as we're both on the same side of the wire. But everything comes down to turf. The United States ain't in this pushbutton rumble because of politics or duty or communism or any of that jive they feed us in *The Stars and Stripes*. We wanted to make our mark on another street. Enough of us had to march that road to prove who the U.S. was. But this country ain't our turf and we're running with our balls in our hands."

"I'm chained to old time doing time," Perez said.

"I got one for you," Fernandez announced. "What do politicians do with a Rican who wants to get ahead: They make a war and teach him how to disappear. Domino War. I'm going to live hard for lost time. The streets are all that's left. Nobody better get in my way."

Priest stood in the dark outside the club—no place to go. The bar was too full of pictures. Going back to the hut meant watching Isaacs fade. He stepped off the boardwalk and went to the closest square of sandbags. A polaroid trophy of a human kill. The picture ticked in his skull. Nothing in his parents' home or in the family albums prepared him. Even the photographs of his father in uniform had kept killing out of sight.

He should take solace that once he had a home where people cared and tried not to wound. But the thought made him feel like an exile all over again. What had happened to leave him without a sense of place?

There he was again—double. He was rotting on the wire, then snap, a rifle at a table celebrating death. Black and white. Other folk saw the difference while Priest was strung out in between. Some people see light, others shadow, a few both at once.

Priest thought to himself, I see the space outside the frame and can't explain what happens. Everything is perspective, the angle of the shot. I don't believe in anything anymore, yet I know people can do better. I can survive without home and the pictures, if I can just feel connected. Not whole, just in touch with others. Priest was terrified that he would die feeling only a sense of loss.

Once Priest believed people could make life a garden.

Now he was not sure. It enraged him to feel cut off from home. He imagined climbing to the top of a building and picking off everyone. If he survived, would the States turn into a bestiary of commonplaces: people fighting people for a place to park? Tired faces dragging prospects on a leash? He had to do something for Isaacs before he went out.

The barkeep and the two gyrenes who were bouncers eased the men out of the enlisted club at the posted hour. Table by table, the men retrieved their weapons at the front and left in groups, not as much for company as to pick up the cadence of numbers.

When Kirsch and the others got outside, Priest came out from the emplacement of the closest quarters.

"Thought you were back at the hut," Hendrick said.

"Just burning off the booze in the open," Priest answered.

Sound slashed the night. A reddish ball arced upward, popped and burst into illumination. Around the white hot core, coronas of color radiated out.

"That was station seven." Kirsch stated the obvious. "Ostrowski's station."

"He's not taking any chances," Hendrick told them. "A short-timer."

Priest put his hand to his shirt as if something were crawling on his skin. The group began walking back to the quarters.

A cluster flare exploded in the distance, arcing a group of green lights.

"That's our patrol," Hendrick indicated. "What are they doing out by the village?"

"Let's get out of the open," Kirsch said, quickening the

pace.

Off to the south, a stream of liquid fire fell from an invisible dragonship that moved across the blackness. Someone ahead was stumbling over the boardwalk and cursing as if the footing were at fault. They got off the pathway and veered around.

"Anyone got some smoke?" the man asked them.

"A few from a C-ration," Kirsch replied.

"No man. Smoke to bend the mind."

"Can't help you," Hendrick added.

"Another fucking night straight."

They left him behind, his boots clattering against the wood.

"There is the unknown soldier," Lieck said. In the light from the flare, they could only see another grunt from the back but they knew. Hartman walked slow and measured, hunched over as if the ground could crack.

"Hey Hartman, hold up," Kirsch called.

"Oh shit," Lieck muttered because he hated to watch what he said.

"Yeah . . . Doc," a voice came back.

At the far edge of the perimeter, at the main gate, headlights flashed although blackout was regulation. The vehicle bore down on them and roared past. The driver kicked on the high beam and bright light stabbed at a line of huts. The vehicle made a tight turn and searched the other row.

"Something's wrong. I'm going to the aid-station." Kirsch took off. The others doubletimed toward the dispensary.

The field phone jangled and Fernandez had the receiver up quickly, as if the noise hurt.

"Station twelve quiet," he reported. "Aye, Aye, that's 0115 hours. Check." He put back the phone as if he could see in the dark. "Madfire goes . . ." Perez could hear Fernandez working at the sleeve of his uniform . . . "in three minutes. We shoot for five."

"More madfire," Perez confirmed.

"Shoot blind at anything suspicious. Pretend you're the enemy. Shoot at where you would be."

Perez pulled three magazines from his ammunition belt and took up his position.

"The first magazine is going out to the Cowboys from the Ricans," Fernandez said as if he were dedicating on the radio.

Perez put the shadowy bushes in line with his barrel. He squeezed easy and felt the slack turn into recoil.

The jeep skidded to a stop at the hut for misfits and the driver ran inside. Isaacs rushed out with him and by the time Kirsch had the battlelights on in the dispensary, the jeep was outside. A man leapt from behind the wheel, the jeep lurched and the engine died. The lights were still on.

"I've got wounded. Three civilians."

Kirsch rushed to the jeep where Isaacs was holding a compress to a kid's head wound. By that time Hartman and the others were there.

"Three litters, Hartman," the medic said.

Hendrick let down the tailgate and Priest leapt aboard and held a flashlight steady while Kirsch checked injuries.

"The kid first," Kirsch told Hartman. "Keep the pressure firm," he said to Isaacs. Kirsch jumped out and ran inside the dispensary.

Hendrick, Priest and Isaacs brought in the child.

"Where?" Hendrick asked shakily.

129

"Table." Kirsch pointed.

Hartman rolled in a cart with equipment. "He's only a kid," Hartman said, as if he were choking.

Isaacs' sleeves were bloody from the wound.

Kirsch took the child's wrist. "Can't find a pulse," he stated after a moment.

"They're only gooks," Lieck commented from the back.

Kirsch took the stethoscope from the cart. Seconds passed. He tore off the child's shirt and listened more intently. His face was sweaty. He pulled back the child's eyelids, shone the flashlight in one eye and then the other.

When Hartman and the driver brought in a woman, Talbot was with them. Kirsch motioned to the floor nearby. Priest and Hendrick left for the last litter. Isaacs could not move.

Kirsch decided to start an I.V. "What's happened?" Kirsch asked the driver.

"I don't know, Doc. A patrol radioed for a vehicle. I was on the road and picked up the casualties."

"Shoot first, questions later. It was after curfew. They were outside," Lieck announced as if everything were settled. He looked at Talbot.

"Where's the goddamn evacuation card with info I can use?" Kirsch was checking the veins in both arms.

"No one knew what was happening, Doc. There was no corpsman around."

"What caused the wounds?"

"A grenade, maybe shrapnel from an RPG. It was all confused. Everyone was jumpy. The kid's bad."

Hartman held up a bottle of intravenous fluid that Kirsch gave him. Kirsch put a tourniquet around the child's good arm and wiped it with alcohol. "His veins are no good. Lost too much blood. I've got to use a jugular, Hartman."

Kirsch turned the child's head, wiped the skin and pushed in the needle. "Lower the bottle." He found the vein and in moments the fluid was dripping slowly because of the head wound.

Isaacs jumped when the woman began moaning.

"Shut up," Lieck told her.

"The kid is her son," Hendrick said. She was looking at the motionless child.

The child's face was waxy and his lips were blue. His mouth hung open. No one saw his chest moving.

Kirsch went to the old man and knelt on the floor. A ribbon of clotted blood trailed from one ear down his cheek. Kirsch quickly checked his eyes, and started an I.V. "He's got a head injury. Shrapnel or concussion, probably both."

The old man coughed when Kirsch took away the light and then vomited on himself and the floor.

"You dirty fucking old man," Lieck snapped.

Kirsch tore off the back of a writing tablet and cleaned up what he could.

"You got three gooks," Talbot said finally. "Bed them down, and ship out the lot in the morning."

"The boy will die unless he's evacuated now," Kirsch told Talbot.

"Those are the breaks," responded Talbot. "There will be one less dink to grow up and shoot at us. I'm not sending men outside the wire on a mercy mission. These gooks could be bait to set an ambush.

"Call a chopper," Kirsch countered.

"I'm not wasting a chopper on gooks."

"I'll take them, Sergeant," interrupted Hartman.

"No one goes, I said," Talbot replied.

Hartman was squinting in the battlelamps as if he needed glasses. "He's just a kid, Sergeant. You can't kill a kid, Dibbs."

"As dead as a doornail to protect this camp. I'll put you on the point if you cross me, Hartman. This is my camp. You settle with me."

"Not a kid," Hartman shouted. "I'll drive them."

"You'll do shit, you punk kid," Talbot yelled. He grabbed Hartman by the collar.

Hartman's fist pulled Priest off balance but he hung on. "Not now," Priest said, keeping his grip.

Hendrick stepped between them, breaking Talbot's hold. "Let's go to the colonel and bring these casualties. Our own people are responsible, right?" Hendrick asked the driver.

"Yes." He had heard stories about Talbot and looked around wide-eyed. "I've got to get back to my unit."

"You're over your fucking head." Talbot glared. "I'm putting away anyone who crosses me."

"I'll drive them," Hartman echoed.

Talbot turned on Hartman angrily. "You picked the wrong time to crawl out from under cover. I'll hang your head on my wall if you push me, fuck your combat medals."

Hartman looked at Talbot. "I know you. I thought I got away."

Isaacs called to Kirsch like a moan.

"Everyone of you gets burned." Talbot's teeth were clenched. "All burned for three worthless slants." Talbot struck a fist into an open palm.

"I'm not with these fools. I don't care what you do," Lieck told him.

"These grunts are traitors—you shame a rat," Talbot answered.

"Too late, we're all too late," Kirsch said shaking out a blanket.

Isaacs was looking at the body saying, "We're lost."

"Traitors and a rat," Talbot exploded. "This one is a bleeding heart, the worst of all. I'll court-martial the rest of you. Isaacs goes to the stockade."

Isaacs kept silent, but he was crying.

"Goddamn you mama's boy." Talbot drove a fist into his face. Isaacs fell backwards into shelves and went to the floor.

Blood flowed: he did not seem to care.

The men closed in around Talbot. Priest was in front of them. Outside the darkness heaved and exploded. Machine guns crackled along the perimeter. Incoming shook the dispensary. "Take your stations," Talbot yelled and pushed through them.

For a moment nothing was clear. Then they looked at each other, and something hidden stepped out of the dark.

Automatic fire was ricocheting off the tin roof of the dispensary. Kirsch was looking at the others, but they were not seeing him. Lieck was on his belly on the floor seeking cover.

Hartman, Priest and Hendrick were looking at Isaacs who was standing beside the body of the boy. "We're lost," he said while blood dripped from Talbot's blow.

Hartman got his rifle and loaded the weapon. "I'll never go home," he said. He started for the door that Talbot left open and Kirsch said, "Hartman. The wounded. I need help."

"Point and Dibbs won't let me," and Kirsch saw Hartman's face and stayed out of his way.

Priest had a grenade in one hand that appeared out of nowhere, and he was looking at Lieck who was worshipping the dirt, face down.

Isaacs moaned as Priest raised his rifle to fire from the hip. He looked at Isaacs then back at Lieck. He slung the weapon over his shoulder and bolted out the door.

"Take care of him, Doc," Hendrick muttered and then he too was gone.

Kirsch tried to get Isaacs away from the boy and on the floor, but he would not move. The woman was keening for the dead. The old man had lapsed into a coma.

The corpsman had to prepare for the casualties and he was breaking out plasma when the rockets started to fall. A blast shook the hut: they never fell alone. "Get down," he yelled at Isaacs and night caved in.

He was walking to the wire in the morning's dead light. The corpse on the wire suddenly came to life and grabbed Hartman and he ate death. All around, Dibbs and Point and the other dead were hung on the strands brooding over the desolation

---

The gunfire was a secret that would not let Priest in. The grenade was the key. All the pictures were ghosts and came to a polaroid trophy of a kill.

The music went high and burst with the rockets and higher still until Hendrick was running down some trash-strewn one way street like knowing how to murder.

"*Cállate*," Fernandez hissed. "Don't breathe."

Perez searched the dark.

"Not even bugs." Fernandez pushed the field phone into Perez hands. "Tell them we got bogeys."

Perez heard the spoon of the grenade flick away and Fernandez lurched. Another grenade was away while he was on the line. He flattened low and two quick explosions reverberated dully.

Perez sent up a flare and then another. He thought he heard low moans and then the flares burst into bright light. Fernandez was firing full bore. The shapes were everywhere and Perez sighted on the one closest to the wire. He saw a hand held rocket and swung his weapon on the soldier. He squeezed and the bunker fell into night.

Perez was sliding on his back along the ground and he tried to sit up. The sky was burning and he smelled his own blood.

"Stay still," Fernandez told him. "I only got one good arm. I put a tourniquet on your leg. Your running days are over, Perez, and I drew my last heart. We're going home."

The last of the seriously wounded was evacuated by helicopter. The dead remained. The direct hit on the dispensary was still ringing in his ears. While Kirsch was unconscious from the blast, Isaacs bled to death. Kirsch and Hartman moved his litter and the medic smoothed Isaacs' body bag because his hands would not keep still. Hartman looked like he would never go home.

Kirsch did not know if Priest had a chance. Hendrick was wounded bad, but would live.

"Where is he?" Lieck demanded. "He's here somewhere gathering flies."

Lieck jerked back a blanket. "Half his head is blown away. A sergeant's pay." Lieck spat in Talbot's face.

"I made it clean," Lieck told them. "Not a scratch and the aid station took a direct hit. Talbot and Isaacs are wasted.

Hendrick is in parts. That fucking Priest took off."

"Deserter? You low life." Hartman reached for his weapon. "Still playing odds."

"No more," Kirsch said, "or it will never stop. Priest is no deserter, he's MIA. He'll find his way back."

The litter bearers had carried in Talbot's body and put it down without a word. No questions. The attack had come from everywhere.

The horizon is seeping red, and in the distance a village burns from napalm and artillery. Inside the barbed wire, bodies lie next to expended shells and people are wounded and lost. Morning appears like a presence brooding over the metal strands. All bets are off. Dust swirls over the devastation.